Glimpses from the Edge

A Collection of Short Stories Chronicling My Indiscretions and Other Infamous Impressions

By

Dan Bruder

ISBN: 1-4033-6077-4 (e-book)
ISBN: 1-4033-6078-2 (Paperback)
ISBN: 1-4033-6079-0 (Dustjacket)

This book is printed on acid free paper.

1stBooks – rev. 11/7/02

This book is dedicated with love to my wife, Helene, for her endless support and inspiration.

Contents

Introduction

This collection of autobiographical short stories is the compilation of many years of sometimes sweet, and other times bitter, experiences that have delivered me to the world I live in today. I cannot offer the tales of great people that have had earth shattering impact on humanity, only my personal triumphs and failures. If my adventures move readers to simply laugh, cry or gain a deeper perspective in their lives, then I have accomplished my goal.

The center of my universe was, and probably always will be, New Jersey. My journeys always seem to start or end there after taking some severe detours along the map of life. I usually return from these experiences mildly wounded, but strengthened in my belief that there is hope for a better existence for all of us.

I began writing these stories in 1996 with the firm expectation that my immediate friends and family would be the sole benefactors of my tales. Through my egocentric point of view, I always got a kick out of sharing my adventures and experiences with others and watching peoples' reactions. The truth of the matter is that some of these stories do not exactly endorse me as the poster child for good social behavior, but I make no apologies. My commitment was to write these stories factually, honestly and try to be as unbiased as humanly possible. If I did something good, let it be told in detail. If I blundered, let it be told in *more* detail. Yes, I reluctantly had to leave out some individuals' names to cover my own legal backside, but otherwise the events in this book are written as I recall them.

There were a great many people who supported me along the way with encouragement and compassion. For those who are wealthy, powerful and influential and stood by me, I am grateful. Those who struggle to get by and cling to nothing but the hope of a better life, but yet demonstrated their human worth through their spiritual generosity to me, I am forever indebted.

Faith in a Violent World

My dad worked as an optometrist in East Orange, NJ from the late 1940's until he finally retired in the mid 1990's. When he started his practice, the town was a desirable, upper middle class community of hard working people who had tremendous pride in where they lived. As the years marched on, the town slowly decayed into the financially depressed, lower class peripheral of the city of Newark, NJ and was ravaged with crime and violence. His patients were mostly black people living within walking distance to his small, unpretentious office that had gone from a once welcoming front picture glass window to a securely boarded up fortress.

Dad endured incidents of vandalism and burglaries as the 1960's moved on and we all feared the day when he would be the target of a violent assault. This was of particular concern considering the fact that he was one of the few white people in the neighborhood, who also happened to be a Jewish doctor, and routinely came and left the office in a very predictable schedule. If this didn't spell "come and get me!" to some angry local bad boys, I don't know what would. It was at this point, as a young man, that I first realized the fact that my dad was in serious jeopardy of getting injured or killed every time he left the house to go to work. But yet, he refused to move his office and throw in the towel.

My mom and I would hammer him on the dangers and the risks he was exposing himself to by venturing into this foreboding, hostile environment every day. He didn't want to hear about it. It was not until quite a few years later that I realized he couldn't turn his back on *his* community. He had decades of relationships with thousands of people that called East Orange "home," and called him "Doc." Most of the people he helped were hard working, family people who probably didn't want to be living in these conditions anymore than he wanted to be there.

The reports of violent crime escalated and by 1966 East Orange had the dubious title of being one of the most dangerous communities in the United States. To add fuel to the fire, in the summer of 1967, simmering racial frustration erupted into massive race riots throughout the country and that is when my dad's community exploded.

The Newark riots crept up Central Avenue towards his little office like an unstoppable flow of angry lava. There was no stopping it, just getting out of the way of it and praying it spared your property. Buildings were set ablaze, stores were being looted, innocent bystanders were being killed and there was nothing the authorities could do to stop it. I was scared out of my mind as Dad scurried down to the office with police escorts nearby and scrambled to toss whatever he could grab into his car. He got the hell out of there and quickly retreated to the safety of our home in Maplewood, wondering if he would ever again see the result of his years and years of hard work.

It was at this point that he came home with a gun. Apparently, there were all kinds of loopholes being done with the law to quickly get lots of licenses out to people that met the appropriate criteria, and that was simply being white. My dad had only one reason to get a gun, and that was fear. He was afraid the riots were not going to be contained to Newark and our town's defenses would fall as the marauding rioters would overrun our community. He would be damned if he was going to let anyone hurt our family. Still he harbored no animosity to the black community as a whole, only to the thugs and instigators who were destroying their own stores, homes and schools. He made it very clear to me that I should not judge an entire group of people by the actions of a few. Somehow, I was a little preoccupied with paralyzing fear to digest these words of wisdom at that time.

Within two days the National Guard was ordered into the riot zone by the Governor and martial law was declared. The military was in charge and were making the rules. They exercised the right to shoot at rioters and this resulted in dozens being killed. At night it was a total free for all, and anything that moved was fair game to shoot at, by either side. At this point in time, the violence had pushed so close to our home that we could hear the endless sound of gunshots day and night. I still remember how the gunshots in the distance sounded like popcorn being made. Every time I heard a round go off, I wondered if it was a bullet that had just ended someone's life.

As an eleven year old, I was having a hard time understanding why people were busy killing each other. I was completely dumbfounded as to why we were suddenly in danger, having done absolutely nothing to warrant these people wanting to destroy us. I spent the next few nights being ordered to sleep under my bed by my parents in the event of stray bullets smashing into the house. This really drove home the reality that we were very vulnerable. It was at this point that my dad sat me down and explained to me that he was going to show me how to use the gun, in the event something happened to him. Ice ran through my veins as my usually passive, mild mannered father explained to me how to load, lock, aim and fire.

As the sun came up, we stepped outside and could see the plumes of smoke etched against the blue sky from the out of control fires. My dad and I cautiously drove down to the shopping area of our town, which was safely insulated from the turmoil. After buying some essentials, my dad's curiosity got the best of him and he drove us to the perimeter of town to see what we could observe. I was expecting to see bodies and burning buildings, but instead found an arsenal of military equipment and lots of soldiers milling about a desolate stretch of what would normally be a bustling business area.

The scene that will be forever burned into my memory is of Springfield Avenue, the main thoroughfare going into Newark, lined with a wall of army sandbags. Perched on top of this shoulder high wall were large machine guns manned by helmeted soldiers. These guns pointed down an empty Springfield Avenue ready to fire on anything that moved. Not far back from this wall sat a handful of dark green tanks with their muzzles trained on the road towards the burning city. Looking down the avenue it was deceptively quiet as the road disappeared over the horizon. But the sound of automatic weapons and sirens quickly snapped me back to reality. The asphalt on the road had been neatly ripped up by the treads of the tanks like a sick reminder of how our world was being torn apart. I was confused and looked for answers as I watched American troops aim their weapons ready to kill one group of Americans to protect another group of Americans. I turned to my dad to make sense of this, but he couldn't.

After a few more terrible days of death and destruction, the riots were quelled, but it would be years before the healing could begin. After a few months it was safe enough to cautiously drive on the main roads through the burned out, bullet riddled areas. As I sat in the back of my parent's car, I was amazed at the degree of total destruction and loss that these people inflicted on themselves. Many of the residents of the effected communities didn't have a place to go for bread or milk for years to come. Not too many businesses wanted to rebuild and many abandoned the community. Even well into the 1980's I would drive through the area and still see charred buildings and lonely walls that once were parts of people's homes sprinkled with bullet holes that covered them like a bad case of acne.

The area slowly came back to life but was never the same. Only a few good-hearted folks came back and tried to put it all behind them. My dad was one of these people and to our shock and disbelief, resumed his routine of venturing down to what was left of his neighborhood. His little office had been spared from any harm, as the riots had been contained a few blocks from him.

My mom and I saw no redeeming value left in this God forsaken shell of a once thriving community. We couldn't believe that he was once again going to put himself in harm's way and do what was nothing short of asking for trouble. We were stunned and scared that he was becoming oblivious to the blatant dangers that were waiting for him.

But Dad had faith that the distrust and suspicions that festered on both sides after the riots would not cause the local black community to judge him by the color of his skin, just as he would not judge them by theirs. He demonstrated his faith by parking his car and walking a block to his office and back, day in and day out, as he had always done. The only difference was a sad one; he now walked with a loaded gun in his pocket and his hand on the trigger. Countless people thanked him for his efforts and commitment to their community. If he knew it or not, he was making a statement that we cannot run and hide from the deeds of bad people. Only by making your presence known can you combat the forces that are trying to push you out. You can't give in!

His faith in a violent world paid off and he was allowed to continue his practice for another quarter of a century until he retired in 1994. He served a community that most others couldn't run away from fast enough. Through all of the violence and tension in his world, faith in his community led him to a long, rewarding career that kept him safe from ever being robbed or injured. While I was totally relieved when he walked out of that office for the last time, I was also very sad. He said goodbye to something that he believed in so much that he had risked his life for it.

Killing Peter

Through my illustrious working career, I always felt that there was nothing that offered the same immediate gratification as a hard day of physical labor. Maybe it's the aching bones and sweaty clothes that I would bring home at the end of the grueling day as a trophy to attest to my hard work. It was kind of like the hunter coming home with his slaughtered prey.

Throughout high school and college I would rely on delivering newspapers, painting houses, building swimming pools and any other manual labor as a source of income to support my always-important social expenses. I worked for quite a number of these years with a high school friend named Peter, who was also easily lured towards having a pocket full of cash. He was also very gifted at being in the wrong place at the wrong time when working with me.

Peter should have learned his lesson as to the downfalls of working with me in our senior year of high school, when I had a

Sunday morning newspaper deliver route. I was responsible for getting up around 4AM every Sunday and loading my car for the first of two trips delivering hundreds of heavy New York Times newspapers. We distributed the newspapers throughout some very posh neighborhoods full of expensive homes with long driveways and lawns that required hikes to reach the front doors. These papers were really bulky and not the kind you could vault onto people's lawns from the window of a moving car. Every week I had to bribe someone to come with me to continuously get out of the car and carry these burdensome loads up to people's doorsteps. Inevitably, Peter could be coerced into the role and my enterprise was in business.

We would be out partying until the wee hours, catch a few hours of sleep and be off to load the car. By the time the sun was starting to come up, we had delivered close to two hundred papers and were completely trashed and hung over. We did all of this for $25 each.

One routine morning, Peter disappeared in to the darkness heading up someone's lawn as I sat in the car with the engine running. Suddenly I heard the sound of dogs fiercely barking from his direction. I knew we had a problem as I saw Peter emerge from the darkness, running with two large angry dogs catching up to him quickly.

"Go! Go!" he was screaming as he waved his hands motioning me to start moving the car.

"I'm going to jump onto the back of the car as you start going. Get moving!"

He made a swan dive onto the slippery hatchback of my 1971 Vega as I hit the gas. It was like poetry in motion as the thump of his body slamming onto the rear hatch of the car harmonized with the shuddering roar of my aluminum engine. A stunt man couldn't have done a better job, that is, until he fell off the car. Since there was nothing on the car to hold onto, he would have needed suction pads to sustain the ride on the back of our getaway vehicle.

As he bounced on the pavement the dogs caught up to him. I was dreading what I would see as I slammed on the brakes and turned around. But all I found was Peter lying on the asphalt with two very disinterested animals sniffing him. It was much harder to talk him into doing this job again for the next few weeks.

As the end of high school approached, we were avid Frisbee players and found great enjoyment in hours of drinking beer and working up a sweat with spectacular tosses of the great plastic disc. Our hometown was where the game Ultimate Frisbee was created. Being a competent Frisbee player was a rite of passage amongst our peers.

On one such Frisbee outing, Peter and I went to a nearby park that was once the property of the Dey estate for a Frisbee toss. The Dey estate was once the home of Joseph P. Dey, the visionary builder who created such communities as Brighton Beach, and was subsequently reputed to be occupied by major mobsters who enjoyed the maze of getaway tunnels built under the properties. Ironically, years later I would come to have a good friend in my music career who was a descendant of Joseph P. Dey.

As Peter and I were in the midst of playing that day, he was telling me how much he was looking forward to the drive to Texas he was going to make in a few days. He was driving the car of one of the heirs to a major publishing empire and friend of the family. Apparently this person was relocating there and Peter viewed helping this high profile executive move as a prestigious honor. Peter would have an all expense paid trip to Texas and be wined and dined when he arrived before being shipped home.

As Peter told me this story, I tossed the Frisbee and he went running for it. Suddenly, his leg disappeared into the ground as his body lurched to a stop. I heard this horrible popping sound as he collapsed screaming in obvious pain. He had managed to plant his foot in a gopher hole as he was running staring up at the Frisbee. The end result was a broken knee and missing this really exciting trip to Texas. Guess who took his place… heh, heh, heh!

You would figure that at some point this guy would have figured that I was out to get him or I was just bad luck to be around. It would be a while before he came to that conclusion.

Painting houses offered many ways to nearly kill or cripple my friend. There was the time I was standing inside struggling with a jammed window as Peter tugged on it from the outside. Suddenly the window gave way, smashing down on both of his thumbs. It was really amazing the colors he was turning as I stared at him through the glass.

"God Damn it! Push down on the window!" He screamed.

So I complied. But unfortunately, I pushed on the wrong half of the window and only wedged his fingers even more. Once he was freed, I think he would have beaten the daylights out of me if his hands were functioning.

Then there is the time he had climbed a ladder that we had hoisted up onto the first story roof of a home, in order to reach the second story roof. All was going according to plan until I accidentally kicked the bottom of the ladder out from under him and it slid down, slamming Peter onto the shingled first story roof. He was covered with paint from the can that he had in his hand and was nearly thrown off the roof from the impact of the crashing ladder.

But my personal favorite painting catastrophe with Peter involved a house that we were painting in the broiling heat of a lazy summer day in West Orange, New Jersey. We only had one ladder, so I set it up to allow him to climb up onto the roof and then I carried the ladder away to the other side of the house so I could climb to my destination. It had to be 110 degrees on the roof and the glare from the sun against the white paint was blinding.

As I was painting, a gnat or some other annoying bug flew into my ear and began buzzing away. This turned from a bother into discomfort as it started to feel like this little creature was burrowing into my brain. I started to lose my balance from the loud buzzing vibrations and failed to kill it no matter how hard I jammed my finger into my ear. I climbed down off the ladder and walked around front and told Peter of my problem. He looked at me like I was a moron.

"I'm going to the hospital. This thing is really bothering me."

He replied by telling me I was an idiot.

I drove to the hospital and, to the amusement of everyone in the emergency room, had the little bug flushed out of my ear with a peroxide type of solution. Of course this took place after waiting for a few hours to be treated. By the time I left the hospital, the workday was shot.

As I returned to the house to wrap things up with Peter and drive him home, it hit me. Oh my God! I had left him on this broiling hot roof for hours with no way of getting down. No one was home, he had no water and I had never brought the ladder back from the other side of the house. I drove up to the house and he was just propped up against the side of the house, sitting there on the steaming hot roof with a vacant look in his eyes. If he hadn't been sitting up, I would have thought he was dead. The conversation during the ride home consisted of words like asshole, idiot, murder and I quit! It was shortly after that that we retired from painting.

The next summer, we graduated from painting houses to building above ground pools. People would go to a nearby pool store that was owned by the local mob and be sold a flimsy shell of a pool that, if installed properly by Peter and I, would give them years and years of pleasure for their friends and family. The catch here is that the pool has to be installed properly.

This job was a back breaker. The ground had to be perfectly even to insure that the water would be equally distributed against the flimsy walls of these pools. The slightest slant in the ground could result in disaster. This meant that we had to clear huge roots, boulders and anything else that got in our way. What looked like hours of work was often misjudged and turned into days of pure hell.

One of our lucky customers was a policeman in a nearby community. Peter and I struggled with clearing this guy's backyard and compressing the ground to insure a level, solid foundation for his anxiously anticipated pool. This pool was 30 feet in diameter and held a massive amount of water. After days of digging, tugging and sweating, we finally believed we got it right. We christened his pool by inserting a hose, turning on the water and telling him that after a few days of filling, he would be able to hop in for a swim. He thanked us as he paid us and we were on our way.

A few mornings later I was awakened by a phone call from this guy. He was hysterically screaming into the phone.

"The pool exploded! I've got hundreds of gallons of water in my basement den," he frantically explained to me.

He demanded that we get our butts over to his house immediately. Since he had a gun, I thought the prudent thing to do would be to comply.

When Peter and I arrived, I almost had a heart attack. We had screwed up the leveling of the pool and the result was the shell giving way, slamming a four foot high wall of water against this policeman's house like a man made tsunami. The force of the water lifted his garden and pushed it through the basement windows as they shattered from the force of the oncoming water. He now had broken glass, dirt, plants and ankle deep water in his once beautiful basement den. His couches, chairs, stereo, television and everything else were destroyed. As I stood there in disbelief I couldn't believe my own reaction. I started to quietly laugh. It was purely a nervous reaction that almost cost me my life.

After the insurance companies settles the damages for the tidal wave that demolished this guy's house, our problems didn't end. We were told that the mobsters who ran the pool business wanted to have a little chat with us, but we declined and kept a very low profile for quite a while. And to make matters worse, the policeman whose house that we destroyed reminded me how I laughed when I saw the damage, and strongly recommended that Peter and I stay out of his town forever. Once again Peter pointed out how working with me had endangered his life and he promptly resigned to never work with me again.

A few years later I confronted him about the fact that he was sleeping with my girlfriend. He didn't deny it and that permanently ended our friendship. As pissed off and disappointed I was that he did that to me, I walked away chuckling. He managed to take away one of the many girls who would come and go in my life as if it was some kind of revenge. But the joke was on him, because he left me all of these great stories, which I value more than any of those girls. My only regret is that I didn't finish him off when I had the chance!

Music To My Ears

Turning forty-six this year was extraordinarily uneventful. As every year marches on, birthdays mean less and less to me. As a college friend once pointed out to me, when you are five years old a year is a fifth of your life, at ten years old it is reduced to a tenth of your life and when you are forty-six a year is a mere forty-sixth of your life. This is why time goes faster and faster as you get older, and years have less and less significance. Years shrink to smaller and smaller fractions of your whole life as you age. My grandfather lived to be 102 years old. I wonder what a year felt like to him?

Now that I have many years of career experience under my belt, not only am I very selective about taking voyages out to explore life's chances, but I have to analyze the associated risks of even getting on the boat! What a departure from the free spirited sailor I once was with a woman in every port and the constant demand for wine and lots of song.

When I got out of college in 1979 with a liberal arts degree, I plunged headlong into a do or die music career. Music had been my first love and I wore it well. As I meandered through my higher education, I was becoming pretty well known as a guitar player/songwriter who could play on people's emotions like they were puppets. I got a hell of a lot more satisfaction and response from my music than I did from any collegiate activity or organized social commitments. I was willing to do anything and go anywhere to be successful. I once dreamed that I was a locomotive roaring down the tracks with music blasting from my engine. There were all kinds of friends and family on the tracks and I just plowed over them and kept on going. I didn't even look back. In retrospect, it was inevitable that I would follow my calling to my music like a moth to a flame.

I started my first band when I was thirteen and quickly found a mutual attraction to kids who were willing to give up homework, friends and the ever-important commitment to being *cool* to simply jam. The irony is we ended up enjoying all of the benefits of being cool and yet, were the farthest thing from it.

Every week, I walked a couple of miles each way to take drum lessons with a teacher named Gene Thaylor. This was in my hometown of Maplewood, New Jersey, a truly good place to grow up, that everyone should be lucky enough to experience. The town was safe, suburban, with parks, a shopping village and lots of upper middle class political radicals and talented artists. Our school system produced people including Max Weinberg, drummer for Bruce Springsteen and musical director of the Conan O'Brien Show, Mark Rudd, former political exile and leader of the Students for a Democratic Society, better known as the Weatherman, not to mention the actors Elizabeth Shue and Roy Scheider. Being in the breeding ground of successful followers of the heart, combined with the ability and desire to get my message out, made it pretty tough for me not to want to go for it. Maybe if I had known more people who tried and failed, I would have been scared off. But success is like heroin; the act of getting it is part of the pleasure of having it.

The drum lessons were repetitious and the first year was nothing more than banging out rhythms on a pad made of wood and rubber. If my mom or dad walked in the room all they would hear was me tapping away. But inside my head, my tapping was nearly drowned out by the deafening roar of my music. I was falling in love with a way to vent my feelings. Little did I know how powerful a medium it could ultimately become.

The garage bands gave way to a basement band that was made up of a wide range of fun loving, well educated misfits. It became not only important to us, but was recognized as a real entity by our parents. We had actual created something that had the ability to affect their lives too. As a result, they spent lot of time chauffeuring us to rehearsals, dances, concerts, etc. It kept gaining local momentum until it was an accepted fact that we were really a band, not just a bunch of losers playing bad versions of The Allman Brothers and Deep Purple.

High school was a great lesson in dealing with local fame and the teenage rewards of being in a well-known hometown band. I always had a girlfriend or two, went to lots of parties and was fortunate enough to not get the shit beat out of me very often. I was protected by the greasers and jocks who normally would have wanted to kill me but didn't because it would have made them very unpopular. It was my first lesson in abusing power and I loved it.

The more serious consequences that went along with the responsibility of being in the spotlight didn't come for many years. These were the days when I had nothing to lose but my pride. Taking creative chances almost always paid off. I had no rent, no contracts, no social or civic responsibility. It seemed as though there were all of the gains, but none of the risks. I noticed early on that people loved to watch a performer take risks and fly without a net. The chance that they might crash and burn right in front of an audience is so compelling and so romantic. So I invented risks. I made my life dependent on the success or failure of my music. It took precedence over school, friends and so on. The risk was simple; I had no back up plan in the works if my music failed.

The risks paid off. Towards the end of high school we had the school system agree to cancel school for a morning because our band was putting on a concert. The majority of our 2700 high school students and kids from surrounding schools would cut school and attend with or without permission. Our music caused change! Also that year, I was given recording time that was donated by a rising superstar. Something was happening in my life that I wouldn't even be able to understand or express for many years.

In college, my first wake up call to the brutality of the music business was when I took guitar lessons from Sam Andrew, the great guitar player for Janis Joplin's band, Big Brother and the Holding Company. Walking up to his dilapidated apartment and seeing some strung out looking babe laying on the only piece of furniture in his one room loft really scared me. I sadly perceived him as a has-been in the making, even at a time when his records were still selling quite well. I wonder how far he had walked to take his music lessons and who had walked all over him to leave him in this pitiful position.

In contrast, due to some close relationships, I was fortunate enough to be constantly exposed to what was on the top of the mountain of music business success. As a result, I experienced many behind the scenes situations with some world class bands that most people only dream of doing. I traveled around with these bands a bit, had tons of back stage experiences and saw what it was like from the inside looking out. Believe you me, it looked pretty nice!

As the early part of the 1980's rolled on, the band went through many different forms and members. But one thing was for sure, it was getting more and more focused. There was an unmistakable feeling of confidence every time we took the stage. I can honestly say that we never didn't win over an audience. Never! It was clear that I was becoming the focal point of the performance. It was time to 'fess up to it. The band was formally renamed The Dan Bruder Band.

Suddenly we were opening up for bigger bands like The Smithereens, Nils Lofgren, Mick Ronson, Robert Gordon and many others. People who were heroes in my life were coming up to me telling me how much they liked the band. Life was starting to turn inside out. Our emotions and guts were being displayed for the public every night, and we were being paid for it. This was a strange world we were living in.

There were some decent offers coming our way and some promising local press. Outwardly, things were exciting, daring and enviable but internally benign creativity was turning to a malignant cancer. Anyone with half a brain would have realized that the band was doomed to failure at this point. We hadn't even reached success and we had already stopped dreaming to live and were beginning to live the dream. Drugs and alcohol were a staple of the bands diet. Women and lying were a close second. The love of the music, which was the force that fueled the band's creative juices, was slipping into oblivion. It was becoming the music *business*.

By 1984, the weight of all of the band's personal and collective problems caused the whole structure to collapse. It was merciful and happened pretty quickly. It shattered dreams, ambitions, friendships and a whole lot of financial investments.

Even though it wound up as a crash and burn situation, I look back on the whole experience with little regret. My dad once told me that he envied me because, when he was my age, he was a struggling musician who was afraid to roll the dice and follow his dream of being a professional musician. At least I could step out in front of a moving bus and go with a smile on my face. I went after my dream.

Heroes

Any collection of stories or experiences would be a little incomplete without some reference to heroes. I could think of many tangents to go off on in this matter including teachers, celebrities and so on. Truthfully, the older I get, the more the unsung heroes mean to me. I'm talking about the ones who impact your life in a profound way for no self-serving gain and half the time aren't even aware that they have affected you.

My wife, Helene is a breast cancer survivor. No, this isn't another story about a strong, courageous person who looked death in the face and heroically came out the victor. That happens to be true, but I'd rather not go there right now. Instead I would like to highlight a couple of the people whose lives intersected with my wife's and mine during this very scary time and made a real difference. Keep in mind that I can only offer you my personal observations. They are simply little snapshots of feelings I experienced, as our world began to unravel with all kinds of terrifying new terminologies and ominous options. Helene has a bag full of her own memories, but you would have to hear them from her to give them the appropriate respect they deserve. So I will stick to my own images.

It was January 3, 1995 when she was diagnosed with a reoccurrence of breast cancer after being well on our way to the magic five-year survival period since she had been originally diagnosed and underwent a lumpectomy. As the years went on we had slowly lowered our guard so the reoccurrence was like an emotional sucker punch. She was given no choice other than a bilateral mastectomy and the hope it had not spread to her lymph nodes. This was truly a battle of a lifetime. So she did what any warrior does before going into battle, she prepared to win.

I can't remember a lot of things that went on during that time. I guess it is a kind of selective memory thing. But fortunately, I remember a few things that have enriched my life, like the freezing cold night before one of her major procedures leading up to the nine-hour surgery she was to undergo when the heat went out in our home. The temperature in the house was in the low 50's and dropping fast as

I pleaded with the utility company to help us. They told me they were sorry but due to the high volume of emergency calls, we were on our own till the morning. I explained that we had to have Helene in good shape for what she was going to undergo, but they simply couldn't help. I piled blankets on top of her and wrapped myself around her to keep her warm. It wasn't working and we were in trouble.

After a few hours of shivering and not being able to sleep, which was the only escape from our fears and anxieties, a midnight knock at the door startled both of us. I looked outside and there was an unfamiliar car in front of the house. I hurried downstairs and opened the door to see a very tired looking elderly man standing there.

"I am with the utility company and I just ended my shift. I heard about your wife's situation on my scanner as I was driving home and wanted to help," he said.

He walked in and asked me which way was it to the furnace. This guy was off the clock, had no obligation to help us and absolutely nothing to gain by driving out to our house after working all day except knowing that he was helping out some strangers in trouble. I stood with him in the basement and tried to make small talk as he fumbled with some tools. I soon found myself nervously talking with him about how scared I was for my wife and the heat going out was like a very bad joke. He was a good man who listened and offered his best wishes. As he lit the pilot light there was a lot more warmth filling the house than what was coming from the furnace. I must have thanked him a dozen times and then without any acceptance of how great a deed he provided, he politely left. He lost some of his sorely needed sleep and gave us a hell of a lot more than just heat in our house. He was rooting for us and gave us inspiration. If he felt obligated to go out of his way for us, no more than perfect strangers, then surely we had a personal obligation to go the distance and settle for nothing less than beating this thing.

Then there was Helene's surgeon, Dr. Rosenberg. He is recognized as a top New York surgeon oncologist and had all the rights to be arrogant, aloof, and full of himself. He was anything but that to us. He proved to be a caring, devoted medical practitioner with an abundance of humane concern. He helped save Helene's life and made this terrifying journey more bearable with his genuinely humane bedside manner. I will never take that for granted and will always measure other doctors' compassion by his standards. But what is burned into my memory is one simple image of him.

After Helene's nine hours of surgery, she was proving to be a durable, resilient patient. Round the clock nurses and narcotics were at her disposal, little of which she used despite severe pain. I would say the narcotics could have been better served to me after I was informed that we now had the nail-biting two-day wait for the results of the pathology report. This was going to be the big determining factor as to if the cancer had spread to lymph nodes or had been contained in the breast tissue. It would be the announcement if the battle was contained or just beginning. It was like waiting for the other shoe to drop. The next few days lasted forever.

A few mornings later, Dr. Rosenberg stormed into Helene's hospital room and was beaming with a smile.

"I have great news! The cancer was contained," he exclaimed.

There were the most genuine smiles in that room that I have ever seen in my life. I know he wanted to hug Helene but couldn't for obvious reasons and I instantly went into a euphoric state of shock. It was like waiting for the jury to come back with a life or death verdict for the person you love, who had been charged with a crime that you know they did not commit. The verdict in this case was innocent and she was set free to begin heeling.

The image that is burned into my memory is Dr. Rosenberg after he walked out of Helene's room and headed down the hall. I poked my head out to watch him stroll away. I saw this plain looking, unpretentious man who had just delivered possibly the most important news my wife and I had ever received and then continued on about his business with no fanfare whatsoever. This image is the first thing I remember after being told that Helene and I were being given another chance to grow old together.

Well, I know I said that this was not another story about a strong, courageous person who looked death in the face and heroically came out the victor. I wasn't telling the complete truth, because I must include Helene along with the other heroes I have mentioned. She tackled this thing head on and was completely determined to win. She never surrendered physically or mentally, in spite of the fact that she could have and everyone would have understood. I firmly believe that her attitude directly contributed to her recovery. Not only is she a hero, but she was thrust into a life-battling situation that transformed many other plain old regular people into heroes as well.

She has gone on to complete three 60-mile breast cancer fund raising walks that have required her to raise many thousands of dollars. She is an inspiration to others, which certainly is a prerequisite in the hero club.

Nuclear Nightmares

Growing up as a Baby Boomer in the late 1950's and early 1960's meant being the first generation to see television become a spectacular medium, the country became conveniently accessible by rapid jet travel, the Beatles rocked the world and we watched as the Kennedy's lived and died in Camelot. Throughout all of these exciting, rapidly changing times there was a dark shadow of doom and decimation looming over the horizon. America, as a society, acknowledged for the first time that we could instantly cease to exist. In the thunderous roar that followed a nuclear blast, our lives, homes, schools, jobs and government could be annihilated in a flash hotter than the surface of the sun. This horror would be cast upon us by the Russians or the Chinese with little warning. America would be left with the fruitless, single option of retaliation, which wouldn't do us a lot of good.

My first memory was being two years old in 1958 and, one evening after dinner, being carried outside on my father's shoulders to join the other neighbors for some major event. Everyone was very anxious and focused on something that was taking place in the dark sky of our suburban, New Jersey neighborhood. I was too young to understand what the big deal was all about, but sensed the tension. It turned out that they were all looking up in amazement and fear as the first satellite, Sputnik, invincibly passed over our country and sent a very profound message from Russia to America and the rest of the world. We were no longer insulated from destruction. Our adversaries had the ability to bring war literally right in to our back yards, without even getting their hands dirty. We had always fought our wars in someone else's backyard, never our own. Sure, there were already intercontinental ballistic missiles and long range bombers that could do the job, but this made it an endless threat from above that could continuously spy on us and rain death and destruction right on our heads. And the worst part was, at that time, we couldn't do the same back to them. The scale of mutual assured destruction was out of balance, and the world became a much more dangerous place than it already was.

Of course, America quickly got the scales back in balance with their own space program and massive buildup of tens of thousands of nuclear missiles. So we now lived in a world that had the capability of total, self inflicted extinction at the push of a button. Maybe it would happen as a result of an intentional act or a possible mistake. It doesn't really matter because the results would be the same.

As I entered grade school we were constantly reminded about the possibility of a nuclear attack. I'm sure a lot of people my age remember being in school and regularly having air raid drills and sitting under their desks with their heads between their legs. I always found humor in the macabre singing of the song "Don't Look At The Flash." Of course as these events took place, it was always done with propaganda aimed at generating the public's confidence that we would survive and our government would quickly and successfully recover from such an attack. Even as a five year old I had a very hard time believing such nonsense.

I remember being in the downtown shopping area of our town after school one day with my mom. I couldn't have been more than six years old. I was playing outside of the beauty parlor she was in when the oddest thing happened. Sirens began to blast and people wearing civil defense armbands and helmets suddenly were all over the street stopping traffic and ordering people out of their cars. As everyone complied, the street was suddenly transformed into a ghost town with abandoned cars all over the middle of what was a bustling street only moments earlier. The entire population had disappeared into doorways and storefronts as mice or cockroaches would do if surprised by someone turning on the kitchen light. When the sirens stopped, there was dead silence and no signs of life.

I had retreated inside to be with my mom as I stared out the window of the beauty parlor at our dead new world. It terrified me that this was the best we could do, run and hide. Witnessing this neat little civil defense exercise forever changed my life.

That is when I started to build an air raid shelter in the basement. It was my little way of saying I'm going to do whatever I can to survive. The hell with the government and their false promises of protecting my family and me! They're the ones who got us into this mess in the first place.

My parents thought I was odd, but cute, and humored me with my survivalist project. I would take canned goods, bottled water, medical supplies, toilet paper, blankets, flashlights and anything else I thought we would need after a nuclear holocaust and carefully packaged it for the duration of the threat. We had a hollow crawl space under our concrete porch that served as a perfect shelter capable of withstanding a nuclear impact. The supplies were put there and I routinely checked on them to make sure we were ready when Armageddon arrived.

It's probably important to point out that I was a pretty happy-go-lucky kid in spite of this looming threat. I had lots of friends, got good grades and could be easily pleased. I just felt this commitment to preparing for what seemed like our inevitable destiny.

When President Kennedy came on television in October of 1962 and told us that Russia had planted a bunch of nuclear missiles in Cuba, just 90 miles off the coast of America and they were aimed at us, I honestly don't think the world realized how close it was to ending. As the U.S. put up a navel blockade around Cuba and stated that anything short of the missiles being removed immediately would be considered an act of war, this crisis became arguably the most dangerous time in the history of the modern world. We were literally on the brink of nuclear war. What made this standoff even more insane is the fact that it was up to two archenemies to come together and peacefully resolve it. If Kruschev or Kennedy didn't blink and back down, this clash of two super powers would not have been defused and somebody would have pushed the button. On top of all of this madness was the ignorance on everyone's part of how thorough and final the consequences would be.

I'll tell you one more thing, suddenly I wasn't the only one in our house taking a keen interest in my cute little air raid shelter!

It's around that time that the nightmares started. At first they would be vivid scenes of fireballs and the dark dismal aftermath of our homes laying in ruin. These were not the kind of nightmares that would wake me up as a little boy crying out for my mommy and daddy, but rather the haunting kind of images that would follow me to school for days, months and years. In fact, these nightmares had such a profound effect on me that I can still remember many of them as if I was just waking up in a cold sweat in my bed from them.

In one dream I had at the age of seven or eight, I am dressed in rags walking through what was once our beautiful neighborhood and now was filled with dead trees, dilapidated remains of abandoned houses, and the sound of the wind whistling through the broken windows. As I come up to our home, it looms silently against the smoke filled sky. It has no front door, so I walk in. There are no pictures on the walls, just peeling paint chips, no carpet or furnishings and the sickening feeling of hopelessness. Suddenly, I am upstairs in our family room with my mom, dad and some strangers who seemed to be in need of shelter. Everyone is dressed in tattered brown and black clothes; no one is speaking as we all begin to huddle for warmth. The scariest part of this dream was the feeling that this was it! There was nothing left to do or strive for, this is how we were going to be for the rest of our lives.

In another of these dreams I had when I was maybe twelve years old, I was standing on the banks of the Hudson River with a group of people I didn't know. We all knew it was only moments before the flash and the first mushroom cloud would appear over the New York skyline, so everyone was hurrying about preparing. I felt odd being alone without my parents, but didn't even have time to care. I watched as others climbed into large coffins and were pushed out into the river. As they started to float down river against the glittering night sky of the city, I noticed that the coffins had windows built into the lids, allowing the people inside to see the events taking place around them. These were not coffins of death, but rather coffins of survival. I quickly and willingly climbed into mine and anxiously waited to be cast off onto the river. As I waited I saw a blinding flash.

As the years of the cold war fade away, the nuclear threat is not as pronounced. This isn't because it has gone away, but simply because it is dwarfed by other miserable possibilities. The concept of knowing who our enemies were and where the threat was coming from went out the window on September 11TH. I firmly believe that it is only a matter of time before a nuclear weapon is detonated in hostility on our soil. I guess for me it is a combination of getting desensitized to these threats and the realization that I can't build a shelter from a terrorist act, as I could do from an ICBM attack from abroad, that have made my response less pronounced to terrorism. Since we are the only super power left, I also think that the odds of a worldwide nuclear holocaust are less, even though the probability of a local terrorist attack is greater. Since one can't defend against an act of terrorism, the best response is to not let it rule your life and make you a prisoner in you homeland.

There is much more hope in the world today than there was when we sat on the edge of destruction in the 1960's. I know that this hope has given way to my having clear nights of sailing through my dreams without having to stop and visit the terribly aftermath of worldwide destruction. I still don't sleep well, but that's because I drink too much water before I go to bed and have to pee a lot during the night and not because I am tormented by nuclear ghosts.

Driving Parents Crazy

Having a teenage stepdaughter who is driving is a very sobering experience. Suddenly, those immortal near misses and wild times that I challenged the gods with are being paid back to Helene and me. We spend many nights waiting up anxiously listening for the sound of a car pulling up into our driveway, safely delivering Lauren back to us in one piece. We trust her judgment, but it is all of the other assholes on the road that cause us to worry. All of my war stories on the road seem to have lost a great deal of their humor and are replaced with the gnawing restlessness that must have been the reason my parents lost a lot of sleep in my younger years.

All things considered, I was lucky throughout my youthful driving career. A couple of minor tickets, some stupendous car accidents that miraculously didn't get anyone killed and some ignorantly lax drinking laws that encouraged stupid behavior were the summary of my road warrior experiences.

Probably, my most celebrated disaster behind the wheel was destroying two cars at the same time without leaving my parents driveway. It is statistically proven that most accidents happen very close to home, but I'm sure not too many happen within ten feet to the house.

I was returning to my parent's house at around 2AM after a night of bar hopping with some friends. I quietly pulled my Mercury Capri hatchback around my Dad's car by using the neighbor's adjacent driveway. My plan was to pull up the driveway, open the hatchback, load in my ladder for my morning painting job and be off to spend the night with the girl I was dating. Everything went according to plan as I put the ladder in and pushed it up against the windshield leaving about four or five feet sticking out of the back. Of course, I couldn't close the hatch, so I tied it down as far as it would go and hopped in the car. I started the engine, put it in reverse, started moving and making my smooth, unnoticed get away.

Bam!! The car seemed to explode to a stop. The windshield disintegrated in front of me as the ladder was pushed all the way out onto the hood of my car. Dogs started to bark and bedroom lights began to click on around our quiet, suburban neighborhood. So much for my quiet getaway. I had forgotten that I pulled around my Dad's car when I came in the driveway and couldn't see it backing out because the half opened hatch blocked my view. I got out of the car to survey the damage and my eyes almost popped out of my head. Not only did I smash the front of my dad's car with the rear of mine, but I successfully impaled his radiator with the ladder that was sticking out of the back of my hatch. The other end of the ladder that shot through my windshield could have decapitated me. Let's see, I was out drinking, came home at 2AM on a work night and wrecked two cars in my parent's driveway. There was only one thing left to do… flee.

I tried to pull forward and unlock our cars but my wheels started squealing. Finally, I jerked the cars apart and got out again to access the situation. I had pieces of my Dad's grill dangling from the remains of my twisted ladder as I got back in the car and maneuvered around his car for my getaway. My folks should have been nominated for two awards throughout this episode, one for not waking up during this dilemma and the other for not murdering their son when he returned the next day.

The kicker to this story took place a few minutes later as I limped my broken car with a ladder sticking out though the shattered remains of my windshield to my girlfriend's house. I stopped at a red light, thinking that was the civically responsible thing to do considering my behavior in my parents' driveway. I stared at the gaping hole in front of me, and all of the glass sparkling on the hood of my car. I looked over and next to me in a car was the last person I wanted to see besides my father, it was a local policeman in his car. He looked back and forth at my car a few times, stared at me with an "I really do not want to know what happened" look, and slowly pulled away as the light turned green. I think he knew the penalty I was going to pay for my crime and almost felt sorry for me. At that point, if he pulled out his gun and shot me, I wouldn't have totally minded.

Anyway, I hope that Lauren has a really boring driving career and when she sits down to write her memoirs, has nothing to tell. Helene and I would get a lot more sleep in the next few years if we knew that was going to be the case.

Lauren's Journey

Notes from 1997… My journey in life started from an unknown port on an unnamed ship. I was adopted in 1956 when I was a few weeks old by my mom and dad, who in every sense of the word are my *real* parents. The relevance of this is that I managed to travel to what I believe is the exact same place in life that I would be at today even if my mom had actually carried me in her womb. The adoption thing is purely a biological issue in my life and insignificant beyond that point. I was always told that I was adopted from my earliest memories and it is a perfectly normal, natural fact of my life.

Growing up there were times I would avoid discussing my adoption with strangers only because their reaction bothered me. I sure wasn't ashamed or troubled by the fact, but it seemed to generate all kinds of annoying questions from kids and adults alike. I remember being no more than ten years old and some adult asking me what it felt like to be adopted. I clearly remember wanting to say "It feels normal, you asshole!" I learned at an early age that people would never cease to amaze me.

As this collection of stories chronicles, growing up was relatively normal for me, in spite of myself. Certainly the majority of wackiness in my life had nothing to do with the fact that I was adopted. My mom and dad didn't have to convince me that I was their son; it was just a fact and never questioned. The fact that I am totally comfortable with this is the ultimate tribute to them and their effort. I realized that my life was complete in this department when I turned down my parents offer to help me find my birth parents. There was no need for me to do so because I was fulfilled. Good work Mom and Dad!

Just like my journey started at an unknown port it has arrived at another destination that has some hauntingly familiar similarities. I have a stepdaughter named Lauren, who has been in my life since she was four years old. Again, the creation of a family that some might say has deviated from what is labeled "traditional." Hey, I am walking proof that a kid can grow up happy and healthy in what might not be a purely conventional setting. That is where the similarities seem to end between Lauren and myself.

Lauren has always had a hard time embracing the concept of us being a family in our home. Despite both my wonderful wife and I being totally and unconditionally devoted to the fact that home and family are nothing less than sacred, Lauren can't seem to join in. A nasty divorce and the death of her father have not helped matters. She is missing the serenity in her life of respecting and wanting to defend our less than conventional family. It strikes me as particularly odd, having come from a similar group of three people who did just the opposite and lived to be proud of *their* unconventional family. But who am I to judge?

I sure hope she grows up and learns to look back and love and cherish what has been under our roof. I know how fondly I look back at my youth and wouldn't trade that for anything, nor would I have changed a single thing if I could. It scares me to think that she could grow up and view her youth as a cold void.

Notes from 1998… Well, its been about a year since I put pen to paper and wrote how concerned I was about Lauren learning to embrace the family and, in general, find peace and happiness with her life. Eighth grade has come to an end and she is now officially in high school… Oh my God!!!!

The weight and importance of her social life is starting to occupy more and more of her time and her emotional reservoir is usually filled to capacity with these issues. In many families this might be viewed as a negative, "Oh my baby is sprouting wings and flying the roost" type of evolution in the growth of a child. In Lauren's case, her social life influencing her development is a good thing. While Helene and I are still annoying to her, she is starting to see the rhyme and reasons behind our demands.

As she has to deal with what she is doing Friday night, which boy she likes or what to wear to the dance, many of the issues that historically have caused friction in our house are dissipating. Her world is expanding more and more, gobbling up social territory that makes our little in-home issues not as earth shattering. For instance, a request to take out the garbage or clean up her room often would have ended in an argument in the past. While it still might happen, the request is much more likely to be honored by her and the issue goes away. She has much more important things to do than bicker with

Helene and I over chores. Heaven forbid, a prolonged debate might cut into valuable telephone or computer time online.

Being truthful, punctual and, in general, not mean spirited to others are issues that now are being taught to Lauren in her own social interactions. She has always been a very honest person, so that has not been much of an issue, but we have always locked horns with her over the mean streak that she carries. But now that she is the recipient of usual kid behavior such as friends not calling when they promise to, lies to avoid dealing with stuff and kids just being plain cruel, she is beginning to know what it feels like to be the beneficiary of ill-willed sentiments. These real life encounters are teaching her much more than my analogies and stories from my past ever could. The torch of responsibility to teach these issues is slowly being passed from Helene and I to the world that Lauren lives in. Our job is to point out the cause and effect of these encounters and reinforce what is right and wrong.

I see Lauren starting to care about our feelings a little more and actually taking the initiative to pre-emptively address potential problems. Last night, a friend was invited to sleep over and join our family on an early morning day trip to the country. She kept Lauren hanging for hours until she finally got her self over to our house a little before midnight. I know the fact that this girl didn't have the courtesy or respect to at least call Lauren for many hours really hurt her, but she didn't take it out on us. At 11:30PM, I woke up to go to the bathroom and heard Lauren whisper my name from downstairs.

"What are you doing sitting in the dark down there?" I said.

"I didn't want the doorbell to wake you guys up when my friend gets here," she replied.

I thought that was very sweet and I really appreciated it. That is what growing up is all about.

While Lauren still has a very tough time with viewing our family as a normal family unit, she is starting to respect it. I hope that one day everything else will fall in place emotionally for her in this department. We seem to be heading in the right direction.

It is the many little building blocks of life that will eventually build a solid foundation of a person. Sure, big achievements and awards should always be celebrated and honored, but it is how we react and what we learn from the thousands of day-to-day events and encounters in our life that will ultimately write the final story. You can't teach someone to be good or to love; you can only show them it is there for the giving and taking.

Notes from 2002… We attended Lauren's high school graduation last week and her eighteenth birthday is a month away. She has developed into a responsible young woman complete with a boyfriend and an extremely liberal set of curfew rules. The bottom line is that she has earned our confidence in her ability to make good judgments. Like I told her a long time ago, trust is like a rope; you let out more and more to a child and if they screw up you yank it back in and start all over. We have let the rope unwind a hell of a lot further than I ever imagined we would, but in her case, it seems to work well.

In contrast, we know a number of families that project their own youthful indiscretions onto their kids, and these poor kids are presumed guilty until proven otherwise. Lauren is lucky I don't project my past indiscretions, or she wouldn't be going outside until she was thirty years old! But seriously, what kind of a message does it send to a college bound kid, who hasn't done anything horrific or illegal, to make them have take random drug tests when they come in at night? A kid like that is being constantly reminded that he or she isn't trusted and better come up with sneaky, dishonest ways to get what they want. Thank goodness we went down a different path in our family.

Over the last year, she has gone through a dramatic positive change in personality. The colder, less communicative outer skin of teen angst is shedding and giving way to a warm, nurturing adult soul. It is like watching an onion peel away the warn, outer layers to reveal a rich, healthy inner core. This is an amazing and rewarding transformation to witness.

Lauren's acknowledgement of the three of us as a family unit is growing into its own form. She is finding a comfortable balance between what she wishes her family life was like and what it is in reality. A lot of the outward anger and belligerence towards extended family has given way to ambivalence, a step closer I guess. She made a very poignant comment in her high school yearbook that paid tribute to her everlasting love for her deceased father as well as thanks to Helene and I for everything. I thought it was well done and view that as a clear demonstration of two things. The first thing it displays is her ability to deal with the family issues in her life and the second thing it shows is her desire to express it. I view both of these things as evidence of being on a good, healthy track in life.

Someone recently said to Helene and I that we have done all that we can do as far as molding and nudging Lauren, because she is beyond the age of influencing with our values and ideas. She basically has crystallized into a young adult version of who she will be for the rest of her life. I view that as profound advice, and since I have embraced that concept, find more peace in our family situation. It is my wish that her journey leads her to the same love and satisfaction I have found in my life. Safe journey, Lauren.

On The Road Again

In the late 1970's, my college years were filled with a number of hitchhiking trips up and down the Northeastern United States with a few friends and myself. These were trips that lasted for a few weeks and required carrying large sixty to seventy pound backpacks. We explored Massachusetts, Vermont, New Hampshire, Maine and some other neighboring states. These journeys were a blast!

As we got more and more accustom to the road and its challenges, my friend Dave and I started planning a more adventurous trip for just the two of us. We wanted to explore the northern most region of the North American continent. While the specifics of the journey could be loosey goosey, we agreed that we needed a final destination. We kicked around several scientific notions including weather, highway traffic flow and finances but couldn't resolve where we were heading. That is when we took out a map of the Northeastern United States and thumb tacked it to a wall. The rest of our scientific analysis involved drinking too much alcohol and throwing a dart at the map. The errant dart landed on what I first thought was a bug crawling on the map, but upon closer examination, I realized it was a God-forsaken place called Funk Island. It was perched in the barren waters on the far northeast side of Newfoundland. It was the summit of *our* Mount Everest.

The trip started out as most, with us carrying large backpacks that towered over our heads and stretched down past our butts. These included everything from tents, shovels, bedding, clothes, food, and all other sustenance for a month long journey. The large backpacks also served as a disarming signal to passing motorists that we were legitimate hitchhikers, not two dirt bags hitching a ride to the next bar.

We never had a problem getting picked up by good hearted, curious people. While they were obligating themselves to give us a lift and become part of our journey, we compensated them with stories about ourselves. We were a form of live entertainment right in their back seats. They were always fascinated with us as if we were aliens who had just touched down in their car and clearly excited to become part of our exploration to Funk Island.

Early on our trip we traveled through familiar roads up through New England, accepting rides from families on vacation, truckers, locals, farmers and fishermen. There seemed to be no social or economic barriers in the types of people who helped us along. Everyone wanted to be part of the story. On our way to Fundy National Park in New Brunswick, Canada an exceptionally well-groomed gentleman in a large Mercedes picked us up. It turned out that he was a powerful member of the Canadian Parliament and was thrilled to be able to act as a grass roots tour guide for us for a few hours. I can truly say that we were giving people as much as we were getting out of this quest. We grabbed a couple of rides over the next few days with a schoolteacher couple from Connecticut who repeatedly picked us up… Wow, repeat business, what a compliment!

As we worked our way into the second week of our trip, one evening we found ourselves in Mocton, Nova Scotia as hurricane warnings were being broadcast from every person, radio and cloud in the sky. We walked for a while on a country road to the rolling farmland on the very outskirts of town, and at this point there weren't even any cars coming by. The wind was getting seriously strong and we had to figure out some shelter quickly. Dave and I saw lights glowing on top of a hill about half a mile off the dark road and we started trudging across the windy, muddy field towards them. They turned out to be the lights from a farmhouse and we were praying the family enjoyed strangers knocking on their door late at night asking to come in.

A very suspicious man answered the door, and I'm sure he had a shotgun nearby. He quietly let us explain why we were invading his home. When we finished speaking, he slowly turned to his wife and children and informed them that they were having guests for the evening. He took a flashlight and led us out to the barn. He said it would be dry inside and it would withstand the hurricane. It was an old dusty barn with a dilapidated antique car inside that was home to a gigantic spider and her web. We apologized to the spider for the intrusion and hoped she wasn't really pissed off and poisonous. We spent the night with her, listening to the barn creak and sway in the ferocious winds and rain.

As the sun broke way to a beautiful new day, a young girl with a basket of hot muffins and fresh eggs awaked us. She said that they were from her family to us and wished us a safe journey. This was the kind of people we were destined to meet throughout our trip.

The ride to the next destination was in the back of a cattle truck with a bunch of stinky cows. After that, we didn't smell too good as we embarked onto the ferry towards our next stop. As we marched on we made our way to the province of Prince Edward Island, a flat, sparsely populated place that was very unspoiled by urban crap and crime. It was a lovable land of farmers, fisherman, poverty and alcoholics. We got off of the ferry that brought us there and were immediately picked up by a ferry worker coming off the same ship. His name was Milton and he insisted that we come to his home and spend the night with his family. Well, since we had no other engagements for the evening, we took him up on his offer. Oh, I almost forgot to mention, he lived on a farm with his wife and eight daughters (folks, even I couldn't make this stuff up!)

Milton lived very modestly with his family in a small farmhouse that was near the ocean. His family was incredibly hospitable and together. It was immediately noticeable that they were not phased by, or interested in modern music, new clothes, cars, or anything other than food, shelter and family. What lucky people, they actually appreciated what they had! The daughters were all over us, figuratively speaking, and were surprisingly intelligent and mature for their ages. The thirteen and fourteen year olds were acting like adults in every sense of the word. The first night we were there we were up late sharing stories and speaking philosophy with them.

In the morning, Milton woke us up and told Dave and I that his daughters had planned a full day for us. After an amazing breakfast of fresh eggs and bacon he had cured himself, Milton handed me the keys to his car.

"I want you two to stay with us for a few days so we can show you around. In the meantime please feel free to drive around the island and have some fun," he insisted.

Oh yeah… a total stranger taking us in, introducing us to his young daughters and giving us his car. This stuff happens to us every day!

As the next few days rolled on, Dave and I got to know Milton and his family as some of the kindest, most caring people we had ever met in our lives. That statement still stands true. Milton explained that he was a recovering alcoholic who had over five years of sobriety under his belt. He explained that alcoholism is at epidemic proportions in the Maritime Provinces of Canada and sobriety is one of the great achievements a Maritime resident can accomplish. He proudly showed Dave and I his five year medallion and we were moved. This is what his life was all about. That night was to be our last night with Milton and his family. But before we left they felt they had to honor our visit with a special celebration.

We were told to put on clean clothes and meet them outside around dinnertime for a surprise. The family drove us to this remote house overlooking the ocean where they had invited many friend and family to meet and greet the strangers from the States. They had banjos, violins and harps playing along with dancing and singing. The seafood was fresh plucked from the ocean and cooked by them in large vats. As the night wore on, Dave and I were stunned at the amount of effort these people had gone through on our behalf. It would be hard to say goodbye.

In the morning as we were getting ready to say farewell to our new family, Milton said he had one more thing to give us. In front of his whole family he reached into his pocket and took out the most important material thing he owned. He handed me his five-year sobriety medal.

"I want you to have this," he said with a proud voice.

I don't think that there was anyone in the room who wasn't crying. Dave and I said we couldn't take it, but he wouldn't take no for an answer. If Dave and I had ended our trip at this point, it still would have been the richest experience of our lives. However, there was more to come.

We weaved our way back through Nova Scotia again and boarded a ferry in Halifax to begin an eighteen-hour trip to St. John's, Newfoundland. It is worth noting that this ferry was condemned by the Austrian government and sold to the Canadians who proceeded to use it anyway. It was big, holding 500 overnight passengers and a couple of hundred cars. A year after we were on it, the boat sank!

We were steerage passengers, with no room to sleep in. We quickly realized that the crew consisted of a bunch of young, free wheeling sailors who were not exactly concerned with boating safety. As the trip proceeded into the evening, the alcohol was flowing and the conversations getting louder. The captain befriended Dave and I and allowed us on the bridge to see how the boat was operated. As long as we were there he asked us if we wanted to see the passenger roster to look for single women. That's my kind of captain!

We spent a bunch of hours in the bar talking and drinking away. There was this one loud-mouthed jerk that kept ranting and raving about how much America sucked and what a bunch of assholes Americans were. Well, after listening to this Ian Anderson look alike (remember the lead singer from Jethro Tull?) for way too long, Dave and I asked this guy to shut up! A major argument erupted that amazingly didn't result in a bar brawl. It lasted for hours until we were both too drunk and tired to continue. This guy was obviously insane and our insistence to debate him didn't say too much for our mental state.

We left the great debate and camped out on a galley way floor drifting across the North Atlantic. I guess it was better that we didn't know that we were sailing right in the waters that entombed the Titanic. How ironic, they didn't survive even thought they were conscious and looking out for danger, and we blindly sloshed our way through the night like captain Hazelwood on the Exxon Valdez unscathed. Suddenly I was awoken to the sound of someone yelling.

"Get up… look outside! You can see Wales off the starboard side!" screamed an excited voice.

We were supposed to be heading to Newfoundland, and the last time I checked, the country of Wales was not in our plans. I quickly hopped up to assess how totally screwed we were and was astonished as I looked outside. There I stared at a school of whales, gracefully leaping out of the ocean. I went back inside to gather my belongings and looked for my brain to start the day.

By noon we docked in St. John's, the capital city of Newfoundland and started to walk off the ferry. A car pulled up just past us, and the passenger door flew open. This was a common way a lot of our rides began. As we walked up and looked inside, there was our anti-American debating partner smiling at us. We laughed about the night before and he agreed to show us around the city. He turned out to be a passionate artist who lived in the hilly suburbs of the city known as The Battery. He let us stay with him for a few days in his small, ancient loft that included no toilet, only a gross water closet.

We went from smelling like cow shit to human shit, but having a great time. He would leave during the day to do his thing and totally trust us with his home. If this is how he treated people from a country he hated, imagine how he would treat someone he liked?

Newfoundland is a strange place with lots of barren land and only a few cities. There was not too much to see so we started making final preparations for our "summit." It was week three and we were only a couple of days away from Funk Island.

Dave and I were devastated when we found out that we would not be able to set foot on our elusive dot on the map. It turned out that Funk Island was nothing more than a rock sticking out of the turbulent North Atlantic and was home to a bunch of wayward birds. We had traveled a great distance and now were nothing more than the Griswalds getting to Wallyworld only to find out it was closed!

As we started to head south for the long trip home we laughed about the Funk Island thing. Who cared, we were having the time of our lives. We hip hopped back through Canada meeting another assortment of interesting people who touched our lives and were starting to get excited about the prospect of sleeping in our own beds. It was still many days away.

Dave and I boarded a ferry from Halifax, Nova Scotia to Bar Harbor, Maine and immediately met two girls from New Jersey. They were hitchhiking though Canada and were starting home as well. They asked us if we would like to camp with them and travel part of the way home with them. The hitchhiking gods liked us that day.

Everything seemed to be going along fine until the four of us stepped off of the ferry in Bar Harbor and were promptly arrested for hitchhiking. Welcome home! The summer rent-a-cop's prepubescent voice was cracking as he told us it was illegal to hitchhike in Bar Harbor and he was going to escort us out of town. I was nervous because I didn't think he was old enough to drive. We told the girls that we would meet them at a specific spot after we snuck back into Bar Harbor later that day. We found them and spent the night together on a cliff overlooking a thousand islands.

The next day, Dave and I decided to stay in Bar Harbor as the girls proceeded to head back to New Jersey. We realized that we had a grand total of about $5.00 between the two of us and arranged to have money wired to us from home. In the meantime, we hung out in one heck of a fun town until our money arrived so we could make it home.

When the money arrived later that day, we did the only thing two traveling fools could do to celebrate; we went to a really cool bar and blew the cash. We got very, very drunk and were telling our stories to anyone who would listen. Next thing we knew it was closing time and we found ourselves out on the street with our backpacks. A man who had stopped to pick up two girls hitchhiking told them to find another ride because we looked like we really needed one fast. Boy, was he right. Jack turned out to be a nice guy with a dog who was camping out a few miles away. He suggested that we set up our tent in his campsite where we could safely sleep it off. After arriving at the campsite, Dave and I proceeded to break our tent pole and almost kill ourselves in the dark. Our host, Jack, was getting yelled at by his neighboring campers to shut us up and his dog was growling at us. Of course, we were hysterical laughing.

Jack made the tragic mistake of inviting us to sleep in his roomy tent with him and his dog. As we settled in, the dog's growl's quieted down and we were starting to drift off to sleep. Suddenly, I felt that nasty old familiar feeling. I was going to throw up. Figuring I had pushed everyone's patience as far as I could, and not wanting to wake them again, I figured I would go outside and be sick. I fumbled around the tent and heard the dog start to growl. I moved more frantically for the tent zipper, found it, unzipped it quickly stuck my head through the opening and barfed my brains out. I didn't think things could get worse until I realized that I had unzipped Dave's sleeping bag, stuck my head inside and threw up all over him. Oh well, so much for a quiet evening.

The next day Jack was surprisingly light hearted about the whole affair as we scrubbed out his tent and that damn dog was still growling at us. We wished each other safe travels and went on our way.

We worked our way down to Boston and stood under an overpass during a heavy rain hoping for a quick warm ride. Unfortunately, we were back in the fast paced urban world and it turned out to be a couple of wet, cold hours until a car finally decided to stop on the drenched Interstate 95. As the driver pulled over, he went into a skid and smashed into the curb blowing out his tire and bending his wheel rim. He was not going to be taking us anywhere. There was nothing we could do to help him and we felt pretty bad. An eighteen-wheeler pulled up to help and called for a tow truck. The man driving the eighteen-wheeler asked us if we wanted a ride so we hopped in with him.

As luck would have it he turned out to be the last ride we would need all the way back to New Jersey. He was going literally five miles from our homes! We talked and talked with this guy and he provided us with the same warm, generous help that almost everyone else had given.

The journey allowed Dave and I to touch the lives of many strangers and for them to do the same to us. In a world that has a reputation for being uncaring and void of compassion, it is a real revelation to put yourself at the mercy of strangers and be helped and protected. The rich, poor, black and white are all the same when it comes to being confronted with helping others. People might or might not readily stick out a helping hand to strangers, but when they do, they receive an indescribable reward. It becomes very contagious and the recipient usually will pass this fragile gift on to someone else. The sad part is that this frail gift can easily be broken in this bumpy world.

Holidays For Helene

Throughout my life, holidays were times of family getting together, a lazy day of lounging around, traveling on vacation or any of a number of other good, happy memories. Holidays had little significance for me, as I was much more interested in the benefit of the holiday verse the meaning of how it originated. Religious holidays meant having to go to temple, which was an equitable price to pay to not have to go to school or, later in life, work. Birthdays were nothing more than another notch in the hopefully long stick of life. They measured time, not celebrating any great achievement. National holidays were always kind of neat, because they seemed to be rich in historic tales of battle, social accomplishments and political impact. I look at it this way, if we celebrate your birthday and your face is on a quarter, you must have done something pretty big.

This is how I approached holidays until I met my future wife, Helene. When we first met in December of 1988, she seemed like any other person who would respond to holidays with worries of how many chairs to set at the table and how much potato salad to serve with the meal. This was somewhat true, but there was an intense pattern of bizarre holiday connections that we would later look back on as some macabre tapestry for her.

Daniel Webster defined holiday as *"a day fixed by law or custom on which ordinary business is suspended in commemoration of some event or in honor of some person."*

Helene's definition should be *"a day when some traumatic, life altering event will sucker punch you and never let you experience that holiday again without remembering it!"*

Going back to the night of her high school graduation in 1965, Helene went to some parties and celebrated with her friends. The morning after *Graduation Day* there was concern in the family about the fact that her older brother, Alvin, had not returned home. Some figured that he was out partying, others figured worse. As the hours turned into days, weeks and years, the situation of his disappearance turned more and more grim. Apparently he was mixed up with some less than scrupulous local characters and either had voluntarily vanished or was forcibly erased from the face of the Earth. It has now been over 30 years and no one ever heard from him again. Whenever Helene thinks about *Graduation Day*, she can't help but think of the loss of her brother.

What made this even more painful was the fact that this was not the first loss of a man in her life. Her father had died when she was ten. She was always told that it was a heart attack, only to find out 35 years later that he had committed suicide.

As the years wore on and she separated from over a decade of a very stormy marriage, she was lucky enough to fall in love with a good man named Jerry, who she met on *His Birthday*. He was already ill with cancer and their relationship only lasted for 18 months until he died on *Helene's Mother's Birthday* in 1988.

It was only a few years later and Helene and I were already together when she was diagnosed with breast cancer and underwent surgery on *St. Patrick's Day* of 1992. After keeping our fingers crossed that it would never reoccur, the worst news came the first workday after *New Years Day* in 1995. She had the cancer back and was going to have to have a bilateral mastectomy. The surgery was performed on *Washington's Birthday* of that year.

Life was getting back on track for us and, in the summer of 1996, Lauren went away to sleep away camp. The day after she came home from camp her father lost a long battle with lymphoma and died. It was *Helene's Birthday*.

Speaking of Lauren, let's not forget the hysterical phone call we received from Lauren on *Columbus Day* of 1997, telling us she had her nose broken after being smashed in the face during a field hockey game.

Well, if all of this was not enough, on *April Fool's Day* of 1998, I was sitting at work and the phone rang. It was Helene hysterically telling me that she was in the Jersey City Police station and she had just been carjacked and kidnapped at gunpoint! As much as I was hoping it was a very sick April Fool's joke, I knew better from her history of holidays. She had been released unharmed and was a lead story all over the television and radio. The police had managed to keep her name out of the press, so she was referred to as an "unidentified, middle aged woman." She kidded that being called "middle aged" was more traumatic that having a gun pointed at her.

As we laid in bed and watched the story being repeated all over the networks, we started to talk about holidays and what they have brought to us. For us it seems that the mundane days of the week are *our* true holidays. Words like "boring, uneventful and quiet" are the terms that we would like to reflect back on for our holidays. Unfortunately, we can't utilize Mr. Webster's definition for all of *our* real day-to-day holidays and "*suspend normal business*" because we would be unemployed.

The Days of Eric

The first night of the opening day of college introduced me to the person who would be my friend, confidant and partner in crime throughout my college career. I was standing on the steps of the Student Union Building at Fairleigh Dickinson University in Teaneck, New Jersey in September of 1974 when I heard someone yell out to me.

"Yo! Are you a freshman?" asked some guy.

He was hanging out of the window of a brand new Starsky and Hutch looking, red and white Barracuda. It turned out his name was Eric and it was also his first day of college.

I replied that I was, and apparently passed the test. I was invited to join these three freshmen for a historic night of drinking and nearly killing ourselves. The evening ended as Eric crashed his car into the staircase of one of the dormitories. The resulting impact sent the majority of two cases of empty beer cans flying throughout the interior of his Hutchmobile. Our friendship was sealed.

He was a tough, but lovable guy from lower New York State who was very intelligent and sensitive, but could explode if a stranger looked at him the wrong way in a bar. We shared a common love of music that ranged from Grateful Dead to Frank Zappa. We also shared a very serious attraction to getting wasted on anything we could get our hands on and being loud and proud of it! Throughout our academic days, we never had a shortage of the hottest woman on campus at our beck and call. Our reckless, obnoxious behavior seemed to compel woman to our doorstep. To this day, I can't figure out if they were with us to be entertained by us, to protect us or to just be naughty and defiant by hanging out with the "bad boys" at school. Who really cares, because Eric and I had a great time.

Early on, while the partying was new and novel, Eric and I aligned ourselves with some members of a very dangerous biker gang, which I will not mention by name to this day. Our relationship started as we were going to testify against one of these animals for viciously assaulting a friend of ours at a concert. We were discouraged from testifying by the police, who warned us that the retribution could cost us our lives. Somehow these guys thought we actually liked them and they befriended the two of us. We were totally protected from any harm due to the fact that anyone who laid a hand on either of us would have to answer to them. So Eric and I were free to be as outrageous and annoying as we pleased. Over the next few years, a weird bond was forged between these criminals and us college kids. There was a time that we actually cared for these guys and visa versa.

The relationship with these characters continued throughout college until the leader of the gang was found with his head blown off. He had set up a drug buy between some South Americans and locals. Unfortunately for him, he decided to rob both sides during the drug buy and the locals turned out to be DEA agents. He went to prison and, shortly after being paroled, was found with his brains dripping down a wall. If he truly did kill himself, it was the most beneficial thing he ever did for society. If someone else did him in, they should have been given a metal. The world was rid of a very scary, treacherous monster.

Eric had made good friends with the bouncers at The Bottom Line in New York City. We routinely went in there a couple of times a week, bypassing the line at the door and getting the primo table of our choice. As we walked in, Eric would always reach his hand out to a 7-foot tall bouncer, and hand him a small package that guaranteed us safe passage for the evening. We saw just about every major act that was happening in the late '70's. Life was good.

We hung out at two major watering holes, the Fairleigh Dickenson Pub and a small, local bar across the street from the campus. The Pub was a great place to drink 25-cent beers into oblivion and wake up with somebody else's girlfriend in your bed. But it was awfully crowded most of the time so we would head out to the neighborhood bar to hang out with the locals. We were very well known in there and even had running bar taps with the owners. They trusted us so much, that on a few occasions we would be partying with them in our room after the bar had closed and the owner would toss Eric or me the keys.

"Go open the bar and bring some liquor back here," the owner would say to us.

That was like offering Jeffrey Dalmer a knife and fork when he had a guest over for dinner.

The neighborhood bar was owned by a father and his two sons, one of who was a three hundred pounder tied in with the local mobsters. He usually had a gun on him and was always looking over his shoulder for trouble. At his funeral later that year, Eric and I were told by his father that he had been shot and dumped under the George Washington Bridge for not making good on a gambling debt. Ouch!

Eric had a brother who was a professor at a midwestern university. We went out to visit him and ended up coming home with a cute little puppy we named Jerry, after Jerry Garcia. Eric and I proved to not be very good parents for our dog. This animal had no alternative except to use our entire apartment as its personal toilet, since we often forgot to take her out. She hated other woman, which proved very inconvenient in our lives. Every time Eric or I would bring a girl home for the night, Jerry would meticulously eat every button off of the girls' clothes! We had to spend a lot of money replacing girls wardrobes… Ah, the cost of love. We were perpetually being threatened with eviction because no dogs were allowed in the apartment, but managed to fend that off until we graduated. Eventually we graduated and Jerry went to a farm to live out her golden years.

One of my first experiences with strangers helping strangers took place while traveling back to New Jersey from another trip Eric and I had made to visit his brother in the Midwest. We were about 18 hours into a 22-hour ride back home on Easter Sunday. It was about 4AM and we were in the Wilkes-Barre, Pennsylvania area about to run out of gas. I got on our CB radio, since there were no cell phones in those days, and started looking for help to locate a gas station so we could dump our last $4.00 into the gas tank. Not expecting to hear anyone come back to our plea for help, we were very surprised when a friendly voice responded to our request by offering us directions to a small, out of the way gas station. Seeing how it was probably the only thing open within driving range, we decided to pursue the kind voice's suggestion.

We made it to the station that was nothing more than a shack with some pumps and saw an elderly couple in a beat up old station wagon standing off to the side. They greeted us and explained that they were the people we were speaking with on the CB radio, which they had been monitoring from their house. They drove out to the station to meet us and offer any additional help we might need. Eric and I looked at each other in total disbelief and thanked them. The gas station attendant asked us how much gas we wanted and we told him to put in only $4.00 since we didn't have a penny more.

"No, fill up their tank. It's on me," said the old man.

I said that that was really nice to offer, but we couldn't accept that. He insisted and we would have clearly insulted them if we didn't accept. We were stunned at their generosity and caring for total strangers.

"I don't know how to thank you," I said.

"You can thank me by passing the favor along someday to someone else who needs help," he replied.

To this day I remember those words and occasionally live by them. It feels damn good when I do it.

Eric and I had a passion for the great outdoors and participated in a number of camping trips. Often these escapades were more trips than camping. There was the infamous time that a dozen of us went up to Harriman Park in New York State and, in the wee hours of the morning, one of our demented friends slipped a tab of something into our sleeping mouths. All I know is when I woke up, I was staring at the inside of the tent that was breathing like a giant lung. It was complete with veins and blood flowing through it. The day went downhill from there. Since we were all exercising pitiful judgment, we organized a game of cowboys and Indians using BB guns and real bows and arrows. It's amazing that we didn't kill each other or at least lose an eye or a tooth.

Enjoying the great outdoors led the two of us to go up to Baxter State Park in Northern Maine for a week of camping, real camping. We were at the base of Mount Katadin, the tallest mountain in the eastern United States and the end of the Appalachian Trail. We hiked endlessly, sat and watched wild moose walk right up to us and stared at breathtaking skies that were so clear you could see satellites drift by. We would talk for hours and hours about what we wanted to do with our lives and about our hopes and dreams.

We worked together in a very upscale, men's clothing store in New York City. It was owned by this eccentric millionaire who designed a line of menswear based on his love for this obnoxious pet he owned. Personally, we all hated this miserable excuse for an animal. It would bite us, growl at us and generally get a kick in the ass from us whenever possible.

The store opened my eyes to many ways to be entrepreneurial and to get our little piece of the American dream. This upstairs, exclusive store often catered to wealthy business people, politicians and celebrities. We would always be amazed at the incredible amounts of money these guys would dump on clothes. We resented that we were struggling to make a buck and these clowns would dump a few grand per visit. I watched in amazement as some of the employees participated in what was a major scam in the New York garment business at that time. It involved mailing empty boxes back to peoples' homes in New Jersey and letting them walk out of the store with their purchases. This allowed them to avoid paying the New York sales tax, and they in turn, would split the savings with the salesperson. Ah, capitalism from the grass roots!

The summer before our senior year of college, Eric's dad passed away and it was very hard on him. I think it gave him a real wake up call to the fact that we are all mortal. That was the first time that I saw him start to mellow out slightly. In retrospect, he was growing up. It would be many years before I would catch up.

That same summer, I started dating a sixteen-year-old girl I met at the local bar across from the campus. It worked well to my advantage that the bar wasn't very big on checking ID. She was wonderful and we quickly were attached at the hip for the next few years. Everybody, and I mean everybody, busted my chops about dating such a young girl, especially Eric. Quite frankly, I didn't give a shit because the two of us were having a great time so the joke was on everyone else.

Her parents seemed to love me and totally accepted our relationship. Her dad was the creator of a world famous rock band. He worked for Don Kirshner, the creator of The Monkees, and was heavily connected in the music business. He had written several hit songs for Leslie Gore and for Elvis Presley. We totally hit it off and through him, I had the opportunity to see another part of the music business that most people never get to see. He was a surprisingly gentle, pleasant person considering the ruthless, aggressive industry he was in. We became good friends.

Eric stopped making fun of me the day I introduced him to my girlfriend's best friend, who was fifteen years old. The two of them fell in love, and after many years got married and are still together to this day, twenty something years later. Since he would have been "the pot calling the kettle an asshole," he refrained from every cracking another joke on the subject.

Eric and I lost touch after graduation and the years marched on. A few years ago I bumped into my old girlfriend who told me that Eric and his wife were now both successful professionals living in New Jersey. My locating him was tempered by the distinct feeling of dread that his wife might react to my attempts to contact him by telling him to stay away from "evil old Dan." I was relieved when after calling him a few times, we all got together to pick up where we left off and laughed at our receding hairlines and paunch bellies. We looked in amazement at each other's wonderful, healthy families and wondered how the hell we ever survived what we put ourselves through. I cherish those crazy memories with Eric and am thankful to be alive to recant them.

The Mouse

Driving down the highway the short distance I traveled to get to work on a summer morning in 1994, I was suddenly struck by the feeling of being observed. I looked around… no cops on the side of the road, no beautiful women flirting with me in passing cars and suddenly there he was, right on the hood of my car! Somehow a field mouse was straddled on the car facing the windshield clinging on for dear life. He was roaring down the highway tail first staring at me with shear terror and mutual disbelief. His hair was blowing backwards over his head and he looked like a reject from an early '60's band. He probably had found a nice, warm accommodation on the engine block during the night and once we got cruising, managed to climb out and see what the commotion was all about.

I locked eyes with this rodent and suddenly we had a major life situation in common. He was about to die and I was going to be the cause of his death. Quite frankly, if I had to set a mousetrap to rid my house of him or his relatives, I could care less. But the fact that he was staring me in the eye made it real personal.

I had a dash of feeling pretty bad sprinkled on my plate of amusement when suddenly he made his move. He started to turn so he was beginning to face forward and I could see him squinting as the wind slammed into his little face. His tiny mouse legs were quivering as his little claws slid over the smooth surface of my car like glass sliding on wet ice. And as quick as he appeared he suddenly took off in a great acrobatic flip, bouncing off my windshield and into the oblivion of the cars that followed me. Before he smashed into the windshield of the car behind me, I wonder what he was thinking. Did he realize that he was going to die or that he was making a final connection with a higher life form that would make great fuel for this story? This little guy actually did more in his little mouse life than a lot of humans get accomplished. He left a strong impression on me and, of course, on the windshield of the car following me.

Just like the mouse, I guess we all have the opportunity to make decisions that will put us in positions to be catapulted to success or disaster. We might slip and slide and cling on to the little bit that we have, or roll the dice and make our move to get to a better place. No risk, no gain is a reasonable analogy. But buying the notion of making your move does not come with a guarantee of success, and the cost might just end up being everything you have in your life. So shop smartly.

Harold

I've always been told that you only need enough good friends to count on one hand. As I went through my school years I had a lot of casual friends and a handful of very close friends. I remember once debating with my father on our front porch how close these friends were to me, and how our friendship would last forever.

"I would die for them and they would do the same for me," I professed to my Dad.

"You can't really be that stupid to believe that, can you?" he responded with his famous diplomacy.

One of my close friends was Harold. We forged our friendship in grammar school in the late 1960's and maintained a close relationship as we went into college. He was a good natured, mischievous kid who reminded me of myself in many ways. We got into all kinds of trouble, some minor and some not so minor.

Long before we earned our badges of honor as social misfits there were a few incidents that were good training for our later years as troublemakers. For instance, there was the time we found some unexplainable entertainment in throwing lit matches out of his bedroom window in the fall of our sixth grade year. We had to interrupt this event when Harold had to go to the bathroom. As I sat on the edge of his bed waiting for him to finish, I caught the sight of a plume of smoke from outside his window. I ran over and looked out to see his family's tool shed roof covered in flames. We had successfully ignited the autumn leaves ablaze with our pyrotronics. I slammed open the bathroom door screaming as Harold sat on the toilet with his pants down to his ankles. After quickly dumping the garbage pail all over the bathroom, and repeatedly filling it with water and pouring it on the fire, we successfully extinguished it. We made up some totally lame story to his parents why the shed was charred, which, of course they didn't believe for an instant.

Soon thereafter, Harold and I followed an after school ritual of walking a few blocks from his house up to Springfield Avenue to go to the candy store. On this particular day, we were loitering in front of the store when we noticed three men standing in front of the bank across the street. We must have been very obvious in staring at them because they took a very serious notice of us as well. We got nervous and started to walk home.

We had walked about a block when suddenly we saw these same men slowly driving down the street looking for something. Then it dawned on us, they were looking for Harold and me! Pure terror ran through our veins as we dove into some shrubs to hide from these men. As their car slowly passed the bush we were hiding in, we bee-lined it for the nearest house, and frantically started ringing the doorbell and pounding on the door screaming for help. A nice old lady answered the door and we blurted out bits and pieces of our tale begging her to let us quickly use the phone. Thankfully, this was a long time ago when people would actually let a stranger in and help them.

Harold called his mother who quickly drove over and picked us up. We hid in the back seat of her car as we explained what had happened. She tried to calm us down, but I think she felt it was an innocent situation that we misinterpreted as a threatening danger. We pulled into their driveway and she continued to reassure us that whatever had happened, it was over and we should start thinking about what she could make us as a snack. We were all walking up the driveway when suddenly a car quickly pulled up in front of the house. It was the three men and they were frantically getting out of the car. Harold, his Mom and I raced into the house in total panic!

As Harold's mom called the Maplewood Police I remember shaking uncontrollably feeling like a trapped animal about to be killed. The police desk sergeant quickly dispatched the cavalry to our rescue. Harold's mom was told not to open the door to anyone unless they used the code word "Tory." This way we could be certain that the person trying to get in was there to save us. The three men were trying the windows and after what seemed like a very long time disappeared into their car and were gone.

Eventually the police arrived announcing, "Tory! Tory!" and we told them our story. If Harold's mom hadn't witnessed this, I'm sure we would have not been believed at all. As it was they didn't seem to care very much or offer any consolation. They filled out their paperwork and left.

That is where we thought the story ended until three men fitting our assailants' descriptions robbed the same bank a few weeks later.

Skip ahead a few years as we were in high school and now were full-fledged longhaired freaks that lived for enjoying life and occasionally getting an education. We were at that overlap point where we would still occasionally do things with our parents, but only on our terms. This often involved us sneaking contraband into the family festivities for our consumption. It also routinely involved making other bad decisions.

On one such occasion, Harold's parents were nice enough to take me along on a family trip to Lake Mohonk in New York State. There we stayed at this well-known elegant old hotel that was perched along side the lake.

Harold and I decided to venture out to climb the local mountain in spite of the fact there was threatening weather and we didn't bother to alert anyone to the fact we were hiking. As we started up the trail it seemed that it would be a mild, pleasurable climb. Soon the terrain steepened and we had to use our hands to grab onto rocks. We realized that we had opted to take the more treacherous, advanced path. After we were practically dangling from ledges with drops far enough to kill us did we acknowledge we had blundered. It was at this point that we were in trouble.

A cold front had blown in as the afternoon was giving way to early evening. Almost instantly the rocks around us were covered with a thin glaze of ice making it impossible to go any further. We soon found ourselves at a point that we will forever refer to as "The Crevice." It was a sheer drop of rock that required a person to straddle with both their arms and legs and walk back down like a spider. Slipping in this process would mean certain injury or worse. There was no way this could be accomplished with the ice on the rocks. Seeing how returning upward was also impossible, this was a classic example of being between a rock and a hard place. No one even knew we were in trouble, so no one was even alarmed by our absence or would be coming to our rescue. Therefore we were completely on our own.

After hours of screaming for help and pure terror we finally took a risky chance and made it through The Crevice unscathed. This was the first time I learned the power of a mountain and to this day will never underestimate it. It was also the last time I ever went hiking without letting someone know my whereabouts.

The next year, a thump of an ink stamp on our driver's licenses gave us our freedom. Just like that, the whole world was within our reach. All we needed was a car.

Since none of our parents were foolish enough to buy us a new car, we considered it a major victory when Harold inherited a dilapidated, old station wagon that had been rotting away in his family's garage. Before we got our driver's licenses, this car had become our imaginary getaway vehicle that we would pile into before school, at night and on the weekends to party, laugh and contemplate the meaning of life. It was in the garage, in that car, that we made a promise to each other. We would meet in the garage at midnight on the year 2000, no matter where we were in life or what we were doing. I would carry this promise around for decades.

We put the car on the road and christened it by piling a bunch of friends into it and driving from New Jersey up to Cape Cod. It was a manual shift relic that intermittently would run and occasionally had parts fall off of it. It was perfect! This was supposed to be a leisurely four or five hour ride that would bring us to a friend's grandmother's house in Wood's Hole on the Cape. The first few hours went well as we bumped along the highway and started to weave our way onto the more rural local roads. Harold's enthusiasm caused him to be driving fast enough to have a local policeman pull us over. The end result was Harold being arrested and taken to jail. We had to go to the jail in the middle of Nowhereville, New England and pay the fine to get him released. We shrugged it off and went our merry way.

Later that summer, we took a more adventurous camping trip in the car to Stowe, Vermont. This was a great opportunity to see the splendors of the Green Mountains and enjoy nature. On the way up to Vermont, the muffler fell off of the car and we had to tie it up to the bumper with a belt. Then the starter failed, so we had to push start it everywhere we went. We stopped for gas and the attendant forgot to put the oil cap back on the engine block after checking the oil. As we were gaining a few miles from the gas station, a thick oil mist started to cover the windshield of our car along with the cars around us. It took a while before we realized the oil was spraying from our open engine cap and by then it was too late. Have you ever tried to wipe hot oil off of your windshield? Take a word of advice, don't. I couldn't imagine it would get much worse, but it did.

Somehow we made it to the campground and suddenly everything seemed like it was worth it. We parked the car on a dirt path next to a serene campsite and set up our tents. The only thing missing was beer and we decided to make a run into town. We all got in front of the station wagon as Harold sat in the driver's seat with his foot on the clutch. We couldn't let the car roll forward because there were trees there. We started to push the car backwards to gain enough speed for him to pop the clutch and start the car, but we were pushing uphill. Harold put the car in neutral and got out to help us gain just a little extra pushing power. The car finally started to gain momentum and then even more momentum.

"I better get back behind the wheel now," said Harold.

As he ran from the front of the car to pull himself around the driver's door to get back in the car, we realized that we had pushed the car over the crest of a hill and it was now starting to roll backwards down a hill, with no one behind the wheel! As Harold barely pulled himself around the door we were screaming for him to hurry up. Suddenly the car door slammed against a tree, sandwiching Harold between the door and this tree with enough force to fracture the metal hinges of the car door and bend it grotesquely backwards.

In a split second, the car bounced back from the springing action of the bent metal door and it propelled Harold free. The car then came to rest back against the tree. I thought it was the end for my friend and he was crushed to death. But unbelievably, he never hit the ground. He stumbled around the road for a few minutes wheezing and hacking like a cat with a giant hairball in his throat. We held him up and were frantically yelling for help as other campers started to gather around to see what the commotion was all about.

Suddenly we realized that his chest was swelling. It was as though he was actually growing breasts! I don't know for sure, but I would say he got up to a solid C cup.

He refused professional medical attention and went the route of self-medication, which we ceremoniously joined him in consuming. At that point, we realized that with the trajectory the car had been on, if the hinges had broken off the door, it would have rolled right over another tent with a family inside of it!

The ride back to New Jersey was like a bunch of dirty, damaged souls limping down the highway in a car with now no muffler, no starter, covered in oil and with a bent, broken drivers door tied on with rope and a male driver with breasts. People were staring at us like we were aliens, which we were unfortunately getting used to in our lives. The freedom that came along with having a car wasn't as much fun as it was cracked up to be.

As our worlds continued to expand, Harold and I struggled to keep in touch as the college years wore on. Finally, he moved up to Massachusetts to continue college and we lost touch with each other. It was around this time that I started to have a reoccurring series of dreams about Harold that would last for decades. In each of these dreams, I would be in some uneventful place and suddenly turn around and see Harold. I would run up to him and say, "Oh my God! I can't believe I'm seeing you after all of these years. It's like a dream," And then I would wake up to realize it was just a dream. I swore I would never fall victim to these taunting dreams again, but continued to over and over again for decades.

A few weeks before New Years Eve 2000, I turned on the evening news and to my horror, heard a story that I could not even comprehend had happened.

An elderly woman was crushed to death in Maplewood Village when a building façade collapsed on her and her husband. When they pulled the couple out of the rubble, they managed to save the husband. The couple had been walking only a block from their home as they did every day for the last 30 years. It had been Harold's parents.

At my wife's coaxing, I nervously picked up the phone to call my old friend and offer my condolences. I had no idea what he had turned into or who he had become. Would he welcome my call or hang up on me? It didn't matter; I had to connect with him. When I called, he answered the phone. It was so strange and sad, but wonderful. It was like we had gone through a time machine and just stepped out of it twenty years later.

I went to visit him, his sister and father and it was truly one of the most bittersweet moments of my life. After we both were stunned to see each other inside of these middle aged balding bodies, we hugged.

Here I was with my long lost friend sitting in his old room that his parents had enshrined, complete with the same Pink Floyd posters and high school knickknacks. I felt like it was 1972 and I suddenly closed my eyes as I listened to “Eat A Peach” by the Allman Brothers, and when I opened my eyes, I could see what we would look and act like in the future. It was at that moment that Harold shared the fact with me that we had another element of our lives in common. His wife had been afflicted with breast cancer, as did my wife. Unfortunately his wife lost her battle with disease.

After we caught up for a while talking in his room, he suggested we go downstairs for something to eat. As I walked into the kitchen I stopped dead in my tracks as I looked through the windows into the backyard, there it was, the garage. I reminded him of our promise that was made a long time ago to meet there on New Year’s Eve 2000, but in the end neither of us could bring ourselves to walk that far back and go into the garage.

My Private War

My life cascaded into a waterfall of different jobs and means to keep a steady cash flow happening after I graduated college. Of all of my many career choices, the one that undoubtedly affected me the most was working on the Agent Orange litigation as a deposition editor. It was the first time in my life that I did something for more than just a paycheck. My efforts helped affect the lives of tens of thousands of veterans who had been wrongly exposed to serious dangers by their own government. I carry the impact of this working experience to this day.

In the early 1980's, as the class action lawsuit was launched against the United States government and half a dozen large corporate defendants, I answered an ad for "Editor Wanted." Being a college graduate with a degree focused on English, I figured I would give it a shot, and maybe get a job that I was actually qualified for doing. It turned out that the Kelly Girl Temp placement firm placed the ad.

Once again, demonstrating my lack of self-esteem, being a Kelly Girl didn't sound too bad. I applied, took some tests and was told to report the next day to this large corporate office building for some undisclosed work as an editor.

I arrived and was directed into a huge room that had long tables that seated at least 300 people. We were then informed we were one of a number of nationwide teams that were going to be coding millions of documents pertaining to the Vietnam War and the Agent Orange issues. The job consisted of reading depositions, medical reports, battle summaries and a wide range of first hand accounts in an attempt to extract and categorize certain information. Everything from locations, weather, hair color, favorite alcohol and drugs, weapons, troop movement, food, illness and much more had to be archived so attorneys on both sides could see patterns to support their respective cases. If we did our job right, it would be possible to quickly access every soldier with blond hair who was in Saigon on February 15, 1969 who liked vanilla ice cream and occasionally smoked pot. It was a massive, tedious undertaking.

The first few weeks offered nothing but blinding, endless reading of boring and monotonous documentation. Occasionally, there would be a battle report that included detailed blow-by-blow accounts of fear, violence and death. At first, we all welcomed this type of reading simply because it broke the never-ending cycle of viewing numbers and statistics. But as the weeks rolled on, these reports started to be more and more difficult to read. The people in this huge room were starting to realize that these were the stories of real people who, "but for the grace of God," could have been them. First hand accounts of watching comrades get blown up and parts of their flesh or organs splattering in the narrators face were not uncommon. Nasty confessions of brutalizing, raping and murdering women and children wiped the smirks off of our faces. One soldier being deposed admitted that he drank a quart of whiskey every day, including days he was manning a massive gun that his fellow soldiers counted on for field support. As a result, he ended up firing on his own troops and killed a bunch of them. Probably, the most disturbing story was an innocent account of soldiers simply having a barbecue. These guys would sit in the fields that were being defoliated with Agent Orange and cook as

U.S. planes dumped the chemical agent on top of them. They would dance and play in it as it fell like snow. The kicker is that they were barbecuing in the bottom of 55-gallon drums that were used to store the Agent Orange. Needless to say, by the time these soldiers were giving their depositions, many of them had already received death sentences.

My good work was recognized and I was promoted to managing the efforts of a large group of these editors and coders. It meant that I had to make decisions of what would or would not be included in our editing. I had to make judgment calls that reduced a soldier's life to a simple "yes" or "no" for being recognized in this brewing legal battle. The pressure increased and I was starting to take the stories and images home with me at night. That is when I started to suffer. I would go home, lock myself in my room and cry. I was forbidden from discussing the contents of our work with any colleagues or outsiders, so I was all alone. It was just my private war and myself.

After a few more weeks, the strain on the staff was very evident and people were quitting and becoming very despondent. A psychiatrist was brought in to be available for those who needed to have someone to speak with, and I took advantage but it didn't help. This was no longer a job and a paycheck for me, but an obligation to all of these soldiers who were lied to and taken advantage of by the United States and a bunch of big companies who were out to make money at their expense. We were their last chance at getting even with these bastards, who robbed them and their children of their health and sanity. I couldn't walk away.

I started to go out every night and drink away my sorrows. It was the only way to dull the pain and make the jagged, sharp images in my head go away. I would end up sobbing and being looked at like any other down and out fool who had one too many.

Since we were not allowed to disclose anything about this case with the public at that time, copying or dispensing any of this information would have been an unlawful act. But as I picked up and read the testimony of one dying soldier standing before a closed-door congressional hearing on Agent Orange, I made a promise to myself to share his story with the world one day. His tale was so honorable and heroic; I could not let it be lost in the swirling abyss of history. He was a victim of the lies and deception of his government, but yet stood up and forgave them for their crimes. In his compassion, he went so far as to thank them for giving him the opportunity to serve his country. Many of the members of congress were openly crying as this high school drop out from a poverty stricken minority upbringing delivered home what the war was all about… honor and pride. In the second day of testimony, it was acknowledged by medical experts that he was dying from massive exposure to Agent Orange. He responded with compassion by saying that he knew he was dying and his life was going to be taken away from him, but there were things more important that were his forever. He pointed up to the American flag and said that every time he sees it waving, the fact that he knew he was going to die for it was worth the price. He went on and on and was scheduled to return for the next day of testimony. He had a good story that everyone could learn from. I really felt like I knew this man personally. But when I turned the page it was blank. He died that night.

The morning the trial was to begin with 40,000 veterans on one side and seven defendants on the other, including the United States government, the whole world was watching. We were digging in for what was going to be a very long and painful trial that could last many months. On one hand, we were happy because we knew we were going to be employed for quite a while, but on the other hand, we knew all of the sadness and tears that were going to stain us every day the trial dragged on.

After reporting to work as the jury was being selected, we were quickly told to put down our pens and close our books. The case was settled. Just like that, our hundreds of thousands of hours of work went out the window. The veterans' attorneys accepted what would prove to be a pretty lame offer from the defendants. The United States and the big companies got off the hook by paying each family less than $20,000. What a nice way of saying "we are sorry for lying to you and causing you and your loved ones to lose their health and happiness and lives."

The war is long gone and the trial has faded into oblivion, but I still have the stories and images stamped into my memory. I have found a way to accept all of the betrayal and sadness that resulted from what our country did to its own people. My own private war ended the same way Vietnam and the Agent Orange litigation did, with no winners, only losers.

Crimes of Potion

I firmly believe that the sharpest double-edged sword in our society is alcohol. On one hand, it is a great social lubricant and supposedly has medicinal value if used in moderation, and on the other hand is arguably the most addictive, destructive toxin we could possibly create and ingest. Until recent years, alcohol commercials and advertisements would stare at us through every medium, portraying it as sexy, fun and a right of passage. Usually, within the same hour the same magazines and television station would have some reference to alcohol related violence or wide-ranging stupidity.

Generally speaking, the trouble starts when the word "excess" is introduced into the consumption of alcohol. Some lucky people can moderate the amount of alcohol they consume and the less fortunate drinkers don't realize that they have crossed the line until after the fact. By then of course, then it is way too late.

My first wake up call to society's intolerance for assholes that drink and drive was back in college in the late 1970's. I was driving a girl back home through Hackensack, New Jersey from an all night drinking party as the morning sun was starting to peek over the horizon. Having slightly more cognitive functions than motor skills at that point, I was really scared that I was going to kill myself or someone else with my inability to stay within my lane, so I was going out of my way to drive very slowly. As I failed miserably at aiming the car correctly, I alternated by drifting onto the center line on my left and rubbing my tires against the curb on my right. In fact, I apparently was going so slowly that, unbeknownst to me, it attracted the attention of the police car that was following me and watching my erratic behavior at a whopping 15 miles per hour!

Suddenly, a police car cut in front of me, forcing me to slam on my brakes. Quickly, two more police cars surrounded my car and I was ordered to get out of the car over the police car's PA system. In my confused state, I thought it would be appropriate to reach for my wallet and get out my driver's license, which I proceeded to do. While my hand was still in my pocket, the slamming of a policemen's body as he threw himself onto the hood of my car startled me. I looked up through the windshield and was staring at the barrel of a shotgun trained on my face. Cops were screaming for my passenger and I to freeze or they were going to blow our heads off! Another gun was trained on me through the driver's side window as they were screaming and blinding us with spotlights. They had made the reasonable assumption that I was reaching for a weapon, and if they used deadly force at that point, would have had a decent argument that they were in fear of their own lives. The situation was quickly diffused as we were violently removed from the car, handcuffed and dragged off to the police station.

After passing the Breathalyzer test by the skin of my teeth, which had to have been an act of God or a broken machine, the police were really pissed off that they couldn't charge me with anything other than careless driving. They proceeded to handcuff me to a chair that was bolted to the floor and interrogate, threaten and antagonize me. At one point, one of the frustrated policeman called me a "Jew' and asked me what I was doing with this good looking girl since I was probably a "faggot." Well, I snapped and went completely ballistic. He was trying to get me to lose it so he could justify beating the tar out of me, and he almost got his way. I told him to eat shit and begged him to take my handcuffs off so the two of us could go outside and settle this like men. Now, I have never been in a fight in my life and I think we all know what would have happened had he obliged. Another, more levelheaded cop intervened and calmed both of us down, averting my demise.

After being released with a summons for my driving misdemeanor, I had to make a ceremonial court appearance to bring this idiotic adventure to a closure. I had successfully risked injury to myself, the police and whoever else I could have mowed down. You would think that this first wake up call would have taught me a lesson, but I just hit the snooze alarm and went back to sleep for years.

As the 1970's blurred into the 1980's, the feeling of immortality on the road was repeatedly challenged with minor impacts, near misses, narrow escapes from the law and many mornings waking up with only blurry recollections of the drive home the night before. Keep in mind that I was not only running the risk of victimizing others on the road, but I was often the victim myself. I was broad sided on two different occasions by drivers trashed on alcohol and drugs and several times had to use evasive measures to avoid obviously intoxicated drivers. Again, logic would dictate that this would snap me into acknowledging the potentially deadly consequences that could have resulted from being so irresponsible. But I used the same moronic argument that everyone else uses, claiming that I've never caused an accident so I must be in control.

One morning in the mid 1980's, I was catching a ride home from a trendy New York nightclub with my friend Donny, after an all-nighter of drinking and dancing with friends. I should have sensed something was wrong when he started the car, went only a block and plowed into the back of another car stopped at a red light. Donny blew out his front tire on impact and we had to change it, which was about the last thing we wanted to do at 5AM in the middle of New York City in the rain. After exchanging information with the other driver, who happened to be in as bad a condition as we were, we went on our way.

I fell asleep in the passenger seat as we drove through the Lincoln Tunnel into New Jersey, stupidly putting my trust in Donny's inability to drive. I was abruptly awakened as he slammed into a highway divider on a highway in Passaic, New Jersey. The car careened off of the divider and ground to a halt on this empty road. Apparently, he fell into a deep sleep as we were cruising down the road. Once again we got out of the car to survey the damage, only this time we were bummed out to see that the spare tire was now destroyed. What a jerk, I was ready to kill him. Since driving the rest of the way home on three tires seemed impractical, we had to come up with some ingenious plan. It was Easter Sunday morning, pouring rain, and all I saw around me were factories and warehouses closed up tight. We argued about what to do and ended up walking in opposite directions.

I walked for quite a while and was getting desperate. I was cold, wet, exhausted and ready to pass out. As I was passing a truck depot, I had a brainstorm! Maybe one of the trucks in the yard was unlocked and had a CB radio that was hooked right to the battery. This would mean that it could work even with the engine turned off. Since this was in the days prior to cell phones, a CB radio was the best chance of getting help. I could find an unlocked truck, climb in and call for help! “Brilliant, purely brilliant!” I thought.

As I walked into the yard, I noticed a small office building. I thought I should knock on the door in case there was a night watchman. This way I could avoid the hassle of looking for a radio and have him call for help. I knocked on the pane glass on the door and an elderly, nervous man responded by yelling at me to go away. I explained that I was involved in an accident and I needed help, but he said I had better leave immediately. I became more insistent, figuring that this was my only hope for rescue for some distance. I banged harder on the window and it accidentally broke. He yelled he had a gun and would use it. I fled.

I walked to the end of the yard and found an 18-wheeler that was unlocked and climbed in praying the radio would work. No luck, it wasn’t working without the engine turned on. At this point it started to pour even harder and I decided to sit in the truck for a while to warm up.

The next thing I knew, my sleep was punctuated by the sounds of voices screaming for me to raise my hands and sit up slowly. I opened my eyes and was staring at the dashboard of the truck. I had fallen asleep as the watchman called the police and they had arrived and surrounded the truck. By his description of the events, they assumed that I was a maniac who tried to attack him. As I sat up a saw a dozen Passaic cops surrounding the truck from the ground, on top of cars and on the roof. All with guns trained on me. I don't think they were expecting my reaction when I said, "Thank God you guys got here, I've been waiting for you!"

Once again, I was removed to the hospitable accommodations of a local police station. But this time I was the honored guest of the local jail for the day. I even got a private cell complete with a camera watching me. I found it odd that I had to remove my belt and shoelaces, but I guess they thought that I actually might fashion them into a means of hanging myself. I now know that they were afraid that my dad was going to strangle me with them when he had to come and bail me out.

Meanwhile Donny had walked a quarter of a mile from the accident, found an all night Quick Check supermarket, went inside and called home for a ride. He went home and straight to bed not telling anyone that I had been with him or bothering to send anyone out to look for me. What an asshole.

Again, it ended in a ceremonial court appearance, an apology to the watchman and payment for the broken window. I could have been killed in a car crash, shot by the watchman or the police and I definitely caused a great deal of embarrassment and grief in my family's life.

I haven't had a drink in over thirteen years and coincidentally don't find myself in predicaments like these anymore. Obviously, the brain numbing effects of alcohol fueled a lot of this type of behavior. I guess I am one of the lucky ones who can look back on it and safely say that I learned my lesson without killing or injuring anyone else. It was around the time that I lost the youthful belief that I was immortal when I realized that this type of behavior could actually ruin or end my life. I guess you can have enough wake up calls to awaken Rip Van Winkle, but they won't do you any good until you are ready to rise and start a new day.

CyberDad

It is a typical frantic Friday afternoon at work and I'm absorbed with trying to salvage months of work on a business deal that is suddenly falling apart. The phone is ringing with people I don't want to speak with and I can't contact the people I need to in order to keep this situation from blowing up in my face. I'm scrambling around the office trying to get my administrative assistant off her ass to help me but, as usual, that is taking more effort than it is worth.

The spiraling workload is suddenly interrupted by my secretary's voice coming through my intercom that my dad is on the line. As I pick up the phone, the affirmative answer to one simple question he has will make me continue to wear the smile that I now suddenly have on my face.

"Hi Dad. Is everything O.K.?" I ask.

"Sure. Everything is fine." He replies, quickly moving to his real agenda.

“Dan, have you got a minute? I’ve got a question for you,” he sheepishly asks.

“Yeah. But you have to be quick. What’s Up?” I reply.

Even though I’m busy as hell, the interruption is a welcomed, momentary oasis from what I have been wrestling with today.

On this day, my dad precedes to tell me that the “little sliding thing” on his computer that you put the “flat round discs” into doesn’t work. He continues to tell me that he is at the “blank screen with the little pictures” and can’t get a certain box that is “floating” in front of him with some kind of warning on it that won’t go away. Being a skilled translator in the language of CyberDad, a quick assessment lets me know the root of his computer problems. He can’t seem to get his CD-ROM to work and is anxious to try a new CD he has received. After a few minutes of wrangling technical terminology into language he can digest, I manage to answer his question and get him up and running.

He is amazed and awestruck at how this insurmountable problem was fixed with a few clicks of his mouse and he profusely thanks me. I have to cut the victorious celebrating short and tell him that I have to get back to work. As he and I hang up our phones, I'm suddenly reminded of the work crisis that has been waiting for me. As I take a deep breath and prepare to dive back into my churning cesspool of work, I pause and smile. I might not be able to fix my problem, but at least I fixed Dad's. Small victories are better than no victories.

When my mom and dad retired to Florida in 1994, I was very concerned about how they would adjust to their new lives. My mom had been a clothing storeowner for many years and my dad was an optometrist. They were both very dedicated to their professions, which meant me coming home from school to an empty house every day while they slaved away at work and many nights of eating out because they were too tired to cook. When they moved to Florida in their early seventies, they suddenly had nothing but free time on their hands and nothing to sink their teeth into, except each other's jugular veins.

The first couple of years were a tough adjustment for both of them. My dad started to teach a driver's education refresher course to senior citizens and surprised everyone by being the more adaptable of the two of them. My mom had a much harder time, being homesick and bored, and negatively comparing her new world to her old one in New Jersey. Amazingly, they didn't murder each other and finally she started working part time in a woman's clothing store nearby. This gave her a sense of purpose, which she had sorely been missing since they moved, and that has since led to a happy disposition.

As they really started to enjoy their retirement, I talked them into buying a computer. Now, keep in mind that they had never been exposed to anything even resembling a computer. They are so intimidated by technology that they still don't own a microwave! My dad quickly became the designated dragon slayer who was going to conquer the intimidating computer dragon. I give this guy a lot of credit for having the guts to tackle it head on at age seventy-five. From the day they got their computer, he has been filled with endless questions and is constantly looking to learn more and more about it. The computer became an exciting technological invasion to their home that has proven to be a lot of fun for them and incredibly therapeutic.

As my dad approaches his 82nd birthday, being linguistically exact and specific with terms and sequence has become somewhat challenging. He has had a flurry of suspected mini-strokes and other episodes over the last few years that appear to have impacted his cognitive abilities and capacity to process complex issues. But the computer has forced him to be on his toes and it constantly demands that he not be vague with his thinking. He quickly learned that when he calls me in New Jersey with a computer problem, the only way I can help him is if he is very precise and articulate. He has learned that ambiguity and vagueness will not arm me with the necessary information to help him resolve his problems. So he is therefore highly motivated to reach deep into his mind for the right words, instead of the easy words. I am convinced that my dad's desire to be computer literate has directly impacted his ability to retain his mental processes. How cool is that?

The fact that he is online and has access to the Internet has connected him to the rest of the world. As a result, they have met people, reacquainted themselves with old friends and been exposed the endless library of information out there. It's a sort of "in home care" for their minds. As long as they don't do anything stupid like giving out their credit card numbers to scam artists or other vermin who prey on seniors, I know that the computer is a wonderful connection for them to the rest of the world.

Most of my parents' retired friends now own computers and are pretty comfortable with them. They yak away about new programs they got and are e-mailing away to each other nonstop. This has given them a huge universe of unconquered territory to explore and, regardless of their physical condition, the ability to never feel like shut-ins. So instead of strolling through their golden years winding down in their learning, they are still ramping up! It keeps them younger longer.

Yes, having a CyberDad is rewarding and gives me the peace of mind in knowing that his brain isn't going to be mothballed anytime soon. So when my world is falling to pieces on any given afternoon and I'm told my dad is on the line, I'm never too busy to take the call.

My Friend Freddie

As I grew up in the safety of a comfortable, self contained suburban community, I began to have a sense of security, and the feeling that I could venture out into the turbulent world and always have the peace of mind of being able to run back home when it got too tough. I lived in a place that was insulated from neighboring race riots that had been so close I could hear gunshots from my bedroom and watch as tanks rumbled down main streets. Our town managed to maintain its dignity, even though it was caught in the fracturing family and social battles that erupted from dinner tables to outdoor demonstrations over the morality of Vietnam, just like most communities in America. This survival only fueled the fire of belief that I lived in a special place that was an oasis from a lot of the threatening problems that loomed over the horizon.

After college I returned to Maplewood and drifted in and out of living with my parents, renting houses and staying with friends as I first struggled with my musical career and then leapfrogged through a number of jobs. Finally in 1984, my parents and I decided to buy into a video franchise and opened a store in Maplewood. I had a friend who had what appeared to be a number of successful stores with a particular franchise, so we bought into the concept and were off and running. Little did we know of the futility in battling the larger video chains and little did my parents know how unprepared I was for this responsibility. It survived for a few years and eventually we went the way of Beta tapes and got out as the monster chains took over. The friendship of the person I knew in this business remained for a number of years and we formed a group of local high school leftovers and an assortment of other over-aged social misfits. There were a handful of local bars that we always congregated at and I'm sure a number of these people can still be found there. Watch a few reruns of Cheers or the Drew Carey Show and you can get a sense of what my life had become.

One evening I was tagging along with a friend to some elicit rendezvous at the apartment of some foreign drug kingpin "wannabe," simply because I was an idiot and had nothing better to do. If I had stopped and thought about the danger of even venturing to this bad part of a town as a white man with a pocket full of money, I would have kicked my own ass, if that is anatomically possible.

Fear turned into surprise as I was reluctantly allowed to enter the small, sparsely furnished apartment of this very suspicious black man who was introduced to me as Freddie. He was not this menacing, cold hearted looking pariah, but a skinny, emotional, animated character that turned out to be a hell of nice, interesting guy. He was a Haitian immigrant to the United States who had found safe passage out after opposing the Baby Doc regime. He was a dead man if he ever set foot back on Haitian soil for committing terrorist acts in revenge against the corrupt dictatorship that had killed thousands of innocent Haitians. He was as totaling bizarre and alien to me as I was to him… this is where it got interesting. His reprimands to my friend for bringing a stranger to his apartment quickly turned into a passionate, philosophical conversation between Freddie and myself that lasted for months. Freddie became my friend.

It turned out that Freddie was the son of a very powerful Haitian politician who was one of the few opponents of Baby Doc to be allowed to be outspoken and live in Haiti. The dictator viewed his father as a conduit to the people and, as the saying goes, keep your friends close and your enemies closer. Freddie was allowed to speak against Baby Doc because his father protected him. While I was busy joining in anti-war protests in the United States, Freddie was starting to join in with fire bombings and assaults on the Haitian secret police, who brutalized the defenseless masses. He was eventually recognized as a thorn in the side of Baby Doc and even his father's power couldn't protect him, so he got out and fled to the United States as they were closing in to dispose of him. He joined the large Haitian community in the suburbs if Newark, NJ and was tied into the very powerful New York Haitian community.

Over the next few weeks, I introduced Freddie to my video store friend who joined me in our marathon debates with him about, politics, religion, race and any other dialogue that would have resulted in bloodshed in most other environments. Eventually others joined in as the bond of trust was forged. On his side he would bring an assortment of Haitian revolutionaries, free loaders, drug addicts and local politicians in the Haitian community. My friends and I felt right at home.

I found it profoundly important to be able to sit in a room full of people that didn't have a clue of my upbringing, or I of theirs, and be able to blatantly attack our mutual distrust head on. Some of these folks had murdered people (for just causes as I'm sure they would claim), burned buildings and wreaked chaos for their freedom. We were a bunch of white momma's boys who considered it a disaster if we missed last call at our local bar. I have never met a more passionate, honest bunch of people in my life, or have I ever felt that I was in a conversation that evoked more truth from me. The effect of these discussions on me was major.

At one point, one of the many racist, anti-white Haitians was glaring at me more than most. Finally I had had enough and asked him what his problem was.

"I don't like white people!" he said.

Well, I lost it and exploded in rage.

"Who the hell do you think you are? You fled a country that was oppressed by *your* own people to *my* land that opened its arms for you, and now you're sitting hear judging me! Fuck you, you racist bastard! I didn't oppress you over there and I'm not sitting hear judging you," I snapped back.

I was furious and he was confused as we waited for each other to make the next move. He was silent and.glaring at me, so I decided to continue my tirade.

"You've got a lot of balls judging me by the color of my skin. You might not like white people, but I hate racists!" I screamed at him as everyone else in the room tried to calm me down.

By the end of the day he and I were shaking hands and wishing each other good luck. By the way, as we made our final parting comments, he pointed out to me that he had a loaded gun in his belt the entire time I was cursing him out.

As the months wore on, Freddie and a few of his close friends were familiar faces in my social circles. There were all kinds of outrageous rumors flying around town about the things we were doing ranging from secretly working for the government to wild orgies. None of these were true but it made for interesting table chat. As the bond grew even stronger, Freddie introduced me to some very recognizable faces in the Haitian community. I was honored and will forever be glad that I was that very lucky idiot who made a very stupid, dangerous choice to venture to his apartment that first night. I guess no risk, no gain.

Freddie was a good-hearted man who could have used his political power and connections to take advantage of the situation. I often wonder why he didn't. Was he content with a simple life, was he afraid of success or was he just caught up in the same small-minded crap as my local friends? His world and mine collided like two huge galaxies passing through each other. Inside each galaxy there were millions of worlds that had millions of resulting stories and relationships that twinkled for a while. I jumped out of that universe later that year and never looked back, so I have no idea what ever became of my friend Freddie. I hope he got out in one piece as well.

Macguyver's Birthday

Notes from 1996… Today is our dog, Macguyver's sixth birthday. It is a time for us to celebrate how much laughter and good feelings the little brown guy brings into our lives along with his sixteen year old brother Eliot and his eight year old sister Hazel, who happen to be cats. Macguyver knows something is up because we are talking to him in even more ridiculous human-to-dog tones than usual. I would like to think that he understands that it is his birthday, but quite frankly he probably thinks the commotion has to do with an impending ride in the car or an extra treat for doing something.

Never the less, we go about the exercise of singing to him and telling him that we love him very much. While animal people can relate to these, and much more bizarre eccentricities of pet owners, the balance of society label people like us somewhere between weird and unstable. You have to be the recipient of the emotional gifts a loyal, loving pet can provide in order to understand why people insist on these apparently silly displays of affection. You would also have to witness the interaction between pet and human to truly appreciate how much we do communicate with each other.

From the time we adopted him as an eight-week-old puppy from a shelter and brought this little stranger into our lives it has been a wonderful learning experience of communicating, trusting and counting on each other. He counts on us for *everything* and we count on him for unconditional love and to be entrusted with our home.

After a while you almost forget that pets are species with less developed brains and, I guess, it is natural to project our thoughts into their actions. What I mean is that we start justifying what they do in human terms with human rational. Hey, no one said that we are perfect either.

But no one is going to convince me that Macguyver doesn't communicate with us in very specific terms. You can count on him putting on his crooked little face right after dinner when he has to go out. He won't bark, but rather stand and stare at us from the next room. If it's a real emergency, he will groan and stare at his leash. He is definitely telling us he has to go out. If I raise my hand and say "wait," he will reluctantly lay down and glare at me until I finish my meal and get up to take him out. He knows what is up.

Most nights before bed we have our "playtime." It involves me looking at him and saying the four magic words "where is your toy?" Well forget it, he goes nuts! He will go into a frenzy trying to find one specific chew toy from his collection of four that he routinely guards and gets very upset if anyone takes from him. We then proceed to have me pull it away from him as he wildly lunges and jumps for it. He can be totally trusted not to bite no matter how frustrated he might get as we play. When I look at him there is no question that he is smiling and in his glory. He knows my signals and I know his. And there is always that disappointed look in his eyes as I climb into bed and realize that I forgot to play with him.

He always lets us know when the house is in "danger" because a stranger is outside with one specific type of bark, and alerts us to the fact that one of his toys has rolled out of reach under the bed with another very definite sounding bark. He has figured out that he can negotiate an extra treat by not finishing his dinner and waiting until I crunch one up in his food to urge our fussy eater to finish. That is when I ask myself who trained who here? He quietly mopes and gets very depressed when he sees me put my tie on to go to work.

And yet through all of this wonderful linking of the minds a simple action quickly reminds us that he is just a little, confused animal. Running away in shear terror from the frightful sound of a paper bag crinkling, fear of reentering a room after the trauma of someone accidentally hitting a chandelier causing the fixture to sway slightly, the monster in the vacuum and a long list of other horrific encounters. Of all the times I wish I could communicate with him, it is the times he is scared I want him to understand me the most. I want to tell him everything will be all right and we will not let anything bad happen to him.

Notes from 2002… Macguyver is going to be twelve years old in a few months. He is getting more and more white around his adorable brown snout, which is a quiet reminder that the years are marching on. It amazes me how fast the time goes. While it makes me sad to know that this love and friendship is way past the halfway point, it also fills me with warmth to have such an abundance of happy memories and experiences with this creature. But you can’t have life without death, and you can't have love without loss. I am going to savor every moment we have together as if it has the novelty of being the first and the preciousness of being the last.

Paper bags, thunder and crinkly sounds are still taboo in his world, and are met with him shaking uncontrollably. It is cute in a pathetic sort of way. He still acts like a puppy and he still guards the same four chew toys he has had for many years.

His brother Eliot and sister Hazel died a few years ago at the ripe ages of nineteen and twelve respectively. They are still with us in urns in the credenza in the dining room. I love to watch the reaction of dinner guests as I point out our dead cats hanging out on a shelf. What can I tell you, I get my comic relief where and when possible. Macguyver's new brothers are two cats named Simon and Harry, who undoubtedly will be the recipient of a short story of there own in the near future.

I hope I get to add more notes about Macguyver's birthday in another five years.

Glory Days

Since I was hell bent on being a recognized rock performer, the second most rewarding thing that could happen to me was to spend a great deal of time backstage at some pretty major concerts. Of course, the first most rewarding thing that could have happened to me would have been myself headlining at one of these shows. That time has come and gone, unless the world is ready for an unknown, middle-aged, white guy from suburban New Jersey.

In 1973, I was a senior at Columbia High School in Maplewood, New Jersey when my friendship with a girl from the area introduced me to her older brother. He was a talented, determined drummer who was playing professionally, but hadn't found his ultimate gig yet. So he was still answering advertisements for bands looking for drummers. He answered one particular ad that, in retrospect, was a wise decision. The ad was for some guy named Bruce Springsteen, who was looking for a new drummer for his E Street Band.

About twenty of us piled into a bunch of cars and went to The Capital Theater in Passaic, New Jersey one evening in 1973 to see The Bruce Springsteen for the first time. The theater was half empty as we sat in the first couple of rows and patiently listened to some guy named Dan Fogelberg, who we had never heard of, and then John Sebastian. They were entertaining, but that is not what we had come there to experience.

I will never forget the first instant that the E Street Band took the stage. The theater was dark and suddenly one blue spotlight illuminated from the stage floor behind this shadowy figure. He was wearing a big, floppy beret and had a wild clump of a beard. The band began to play a song called "Incident on 57TH Street" and my life changed forever. I remember turning to my friend and telling her that her brother had become part of something bigger than we had ever dreamed of in our lives. If only I knew how prophetic those words would be.

Well, of course, we all know that Springsteen catapulted into echelons of stardom that few performers ever get to visit. It is my opinion, along with the majority of the rest of the free world, that all of the success was well deserved. I was fortunate enough to experience a great deal of first hand, behind the scenes experiences of what went on at quite a number of these shows, and the shows of a good many other established rock artists. I would love to share lots of details, but quite frankly I was allowed into a private area of certain people's lives who I still hold dearly to me, so as much as I would love to talk, I simply won't. Sorry, friendship is thicker than ink! I was once even approached by a reported who offered me money to discuss what I knew. Needless to say, I told him to go to Hell. Shame on him!

But what I will say, in the very generic sense of what I observed of the various rock acts backstage, is that aside from fueling my desires for success even further, it enriched my life with unbelievable encounters and experiences most could only dream of witnessing. I am not talking about wild free-for-alls and orgies of sex and drugs, because I never witnessed anything like that backstage at any major artist's performance. What I am referring to is the amazing amount of professionalism, commitment and order in which these massive events were pulled off, night after night. The other incredible balancing act was how total pandemonium would be churning outside of an arena or in the audience, but yet backstage there was always a sense of family and structure for any of these acts. It was incredibly organized and insulated from the chaos lurking on the other side of the curtain.

If there was anything I wish I gleaned from that experience, it was that the stage act is just that, an act. When the show is over and the audience leaves, the people who were performing deal with exhaustion, hunger, happiness, sadness and everything else that real live human beings experience. But unfortunately, I missed the message and tried to live the rock life, which cost me my chance at a successful career and damn near killed me. Another thing I quickly learned was that the higher one went up in the hierarchy of stardom, the more protective they became of their privacy, and the privacy of their families. They had to insulate themselves from the lunatic fringe who wouldn't hesitate at lunging at them, bothering them or worse. They would often have to travel under assumed names, use decoys to duck the press, hire bodyguards and be excruciatingly careful of what they were seen doing in public. It was far from the fun and games one would imagine a star gets to enjoy, and is a serious price they have to pay for the upside of their success. I was once accompanying the elderly mother of a band member of a world famous act as we were departing a giant arena. We were coming out of a secret tunnel under the arena that was used by celebrities to make their safe getaways from the throngs of fans. As we left the tunnel, a group of overly enthusiastic fans mistook her for the mother of the band's front man and began to ask her for autographs. When she denied being the front man's mother, the people didn't believe her and got belligerent. It got pretty scary but we made it out of there safely. I would venture to guess that these people were just ordinary, average people who got momentarily blinded by the enthusiasm of the moment. The problems get a hell of a lot more frightening when they are not just ordinary, average people. This is why people in the spotlight have to guard their privacy.

To this day, I sit in the audience at any major music event and am in awe of how smoothly the performances are pulled off. Anyone who has seen the amount of equipment, cables, lights, food, personnel, coordination and dedication these folks worked with, knows what I mean. But let's not slight the lesser-recognized bands, like the ones who fill up theaters instead of football stadiums. These artists have to do a lot more of their own grunge work and usually get to experience very few of the frills. It's usually sleeping on a bus instead of a nice hotel and fast food verse filet mignon. They don't have all of the roadies and support teams to assist them, and often are pooped out long before the show starts from all of the physical labor they have to endure. It is like the minor leagues verse the majors, but they are driven by their love for their music. But when it comes time to hit the stage, there is the same passion and resolve from these types of bands as one would find in the larger acts. Commitment is commitment, pure and simple.

Speaking of commitment, I have a close friend named Herb, who I admire more than most, who has risen from a pretty tough childhood and landed on his feet, over and over again. He has played drums with lots of major acts including Edgar Winter and Leon Russell and has had a steady gig with a world-class country star for many years. Considering that he spent the majority of my senior year in high school living in people's basements in New Jersey because he had no where else to go, I am immensely proud of him and how he has persevered. I suspect that he actually appreciates his glory days more than most people because he has seen much more of the negative alternatives. Those who work hard tend to value what they have more then those who have things handed to them. Most of the people I have known who have been successful in the music business have worked feverishly at their craft.

I remember standing at The Ritz in New York City in the mid 1980's and was beaming with pride as I watched him doing the drum solo in the song "Frankenstein" with Edgar Winter. There he was, the same guy who we wouldn't even let jam with as kids, kicking some serious ass on stage to a sold out crowd. I have witnessed many poignant moments on stage over the years, but this one was sweet and personal, kind of like a rags to riches moment, minus the financial riches! I get more excited about moments like that than I do about most other things, because I watched him from the starting line. I was there when the gun went off and his race began, and now twenty-something years later he is still going at full speed. More power to him! I often wonder what it must be like to be lucky enough to do what you truly love for a living; to get up day after day and say today is another glory day.

I was also invited several times by a good man named Wally, to visit with the band he helped create called Kansas. These guys were just a nice bunch of wide-eyed boys from Kansas who were taken under the wing of some powerful industry professionals and catapulted into stardom. At first, they didn't have a lot of experience in the "big city" and were protected from being gobbled up by all of the sharks and scoundrels. I remember being backstage with Wally and laughing about how you can take the country out of the boy, blah blah blah. I learned a lot from him about balancing life and career, but as usual, didn't bother to apply it to myself. He was the first person to show me what the music management side of the world was thinking. There is an old "us and them" belief in the industry with "us" being the musicians and "them" being the management. It was very insightful to be close to one of "them" and get a sense of the other side of the coin.

I was lucky enough in my music career to have a handful of my own glory days. There were really only two kinds of them; the live ones in front of an audience that offered immediate gratification, and the ones in the studio that you grind away at and often can't even appreciate until you reflect back on them months later. One of the first in my life was in high school when I was handed some professional recording time, which I discussed in an earlier story. I was a wide-eyed kid who suddenly got to see how records were made. I was overwhelmed by the equipment and technical expertise of the guys in the control room and struggled to keep my focus on my efforts in the isolation booth. It felt good, even though the finished product was pretty much of a joke. As the years rolled on, I collected memories of a handful of truly glorious studio moments surrounded by gifted, talented artists that I will forever cherish. But the live glory days stand out as the most poignant moments of performing. As a good friend, and fellow band member, used to point out to me there are times when it all clicks, and it creates the magic. I feel fulfilled that I was fortunate enough to even have a handful of these moments. The strangest part of these magic moments is when you instantly lock eyes with your band members, and your mutual expressions acknowledge that you struck artistic pay dirt. No words are spoken, but the smiles and approving nods transcend the deafening music and glaring lights.

As my band began opening up for bigger acts such as The Smithereens, Mick Ronsen, Nils Lofgren and Robert Gordon, we were expecting to be embraced by our headlining acts like a big brother would do for his kid brother. To my surprise, and the surprise of my fellow band members and crew, we didn't always get the friendly welcoming committee from some of these bands. Talk about magic moments, on one occasion we opened for a really famous band and we brought down the house! We knew it, the audience definitely knew it and the headlining band furiously acknowledged it. The manager for the other band blasted us and swore we would never set foot on the same stage with his band again. Our crime was that we overshadowed them and made them look bad. Talk about back handed compliments! Believe it or not, we had another manager of an even more famous band that we opened up for tell us the exact same thing! What the hell was wrong with this picture, we were too good? I never did, and never will, apologize for trying my best, and to this day do not understand why a famous band wouldn't want the best opening act possible. Even if the opening band outshines them, it shows that they are keeping good company.

I also suffered the humiliation of trying too hard and artistically falling flat on my musical face. I was lucky enough to get my band invited to play at Big Man's, a club owned by Clarence Clemons. The kicker is that it was Bruce Springsteen's birthday and he was going to be there. Needless to say, our band was pumped up and chomping at the bit to get on stage. To make a long story short, we overcompensated, poorly executed, disconnected and self destructed in front of one of my true musical heroes. I was licking my wounds for a long time after that night.

Since those days, I have drifted further and further away from the music business and am left with some rich memories of my glory days as an audience member and as a struggling musician. There is something almost mystical about the deafening roar of a crowd that erupts as any one of our heroes take the stage, may it be the memory of the crowds screaming "Jerry!" at a Grateful Dead concert or the famous "booing" sound that people mistakenly think they are hearing at a Springsteen concert, only to realize that it is the crowd shouting

"Bruuuce!" I can lay in bed on any given night and almost think that I am hearing the ringing in my ears that would haunt me after so many of these deafeningly loud shows. It doesn't bother me, instead it buts a smile on my face.

Well that was then and this is now. For many years, I bored my wife with way too many of my stories and always told her, amongst my dreams, I wanted to see Jimi Hendrix and Duane Allman, as well as have the E Street Band reunite so I could bring her to a show. Yeah, yeah yeah, I know the Hendrix and Allman thing are a bit of a cosmic stretch, but at least I got to fulfill the E Street Band dream a few years ago. As we stood in the crowd at New Jersey's Continental Arena cheering with the masses, I simply loved it. I think my wife loved the smile on my face even more.

Guns

Throughout my life I had a distant fascination with guns. Growing up in a world that encouraged playing cowboys and Indians, cops and robbers, war or any other of the great many shoot 'em up games certainly promoted the legitimacy and social acceptability of the shiny symbols of manhood. Yet, as us little boys in the suburbs of the 1950s and 1960s grew into young men, we weren't running around blowing each other's brains out with vacant stares like it was a video game.

Suddenly, it became a social taboo for toy guns to be used as a means of entertainment because they were deemed to represent an unacceptable level of violence. Of course, now the very kids who would be innocently having a healthy game of shoot 'em up outside are now glued to the TV watching the graphic bloodshed and violent behavior of the WWF or someone eating giant cockroaches for a million dollar prize. And all the while, kids are growing more and more prone to settling an argument by pulling a trigger and ending a life instead of an old-fashioned fistfight, that rarely does more than a black eye or a broken nose. I have two young relatives who were attending Columbine High School the day Dylan Klebold and Eric Harris shot their way into infamy and I don't think that they would be so impressed with how society has made people more responsible with guns. There will always be guns and always be violent incidents caused by the use of guns… always.

The first time I held a gun was when my father brought home a pistol during the Newark race riots of 1967. I was eleven years old and, needless to say, was very impressed with the opportunity to hold a real weapon. My dad's status as being cool rose significantly in my mind when he fired off a round in the basement. Of course, this was an idiotic, reckless and illegal thing to do, but to an eleven-year-old boy it catapulted my dad to hero status. Fortunately, he never had to use the weapon to defend himself or our family and he kept it in his possession until he suffered what we believe was a mini-stroke thirty years later. It broke my heart to have to sit by his bedside and confront him with the fact that I was taking the gun away from him for fear that he might have a lapse of judgment with horrible consequences. To my surprise he didn't resist and we have never looked back on that event with sorrow. By the way, I never once took hold of the gun as I grew up, even thought I knew its location the entire time. I feel that there was no mystery or allure to compel me to do so, since my dad made it a common part of my home life. There was no novelty to going near it and I certainly understood its awesome potential from having seeing it being fired.

My first taste of the devastating power of a gun came at the beginning of the summer before I started college. I was awakened by a phone call from my Uncle Dick telling me to brace myself for some terrible news. When I heard his words I got very frightened, because my parents had left for a trip to Israel only hours earlier and I thought they had died in a plane crash.

"Your cousin Jeffery has been shot and killed in a robbery," said Uncle Dick.

"Oh no! How did that happen?" I replied in stunned disbelief.

"He was working his summer job on an ice cream truck in the Bronx and he attempted to fight off some robbers. He was shot three times in the chest with a 357 Magnum," he explained.

"That's horrible. How are Aunt Shirley and Uncle Herb and the kids?" I inquired.

"I don't know, but it must be awful. Listen, the funeral is tomorrow on Long Island and I hope you can make it," said Uncle Dick.

"Of course," I quickly answered.

"Please do not tell your parents about this when they call. There is no way they could get back from Israel in time for the funeral and there is no reason to ruin their trip since them returning cannot help the situation," said Uncle Dick.

"I don't know about that. They will be furious at me for not telling them until they get home," I replied.

"Please, we have discussed it and this is really what we feel is best. Please don't tell them," he begged.

I ended up not telling my parents for the ten days until they returned home. I must have been a really good liar because they were completely sucker punched by the news when I sat them down as soon as they returned home. It was excruciatingly painful to watch their faces in shock and horror as I broke the news to them.

During college I saw bikers and hoodlums displaying illegal weapons like they were badges of honor. I witnessed these sightings at concerts, bars and, unfortunately on two occasions, in the commission of crimes.

The first violent use of a gun I witnessed occurred as a worked at a part time job in the Bergen Mall in Paramus, NJ during my junior year of college. I was standing in the entrance of the ski shop I work in and watched the crowds of people moving through the main concourse of the mall. Suddenly, without warning, a shot rang out. The entire population of the mall collapsed upon each other. It was like someone had kicked out the legs of the several hundred people in front of me and they were all toppled, instantly laying on top of each other like giant dolls that were strewn around. To my surprise, the only person I saw left standing was holding a smoking gun, with an eerie composed expression on his face. This neatly dressed, middle-aged man turned around with the gun still held high and calmly began walking towards the security office of the mall. I later found out that he simply walked in to the office, put down the gun and surrendered.

Suddenly I was snapped back to people beginning to scream and sob and slowly the crowd's attention began to gravitate towards a man rolling around on the floor. As I made my way through the crowd, I could see he was holding his face as huge amounts of bright red blood streamed out between his fingers. It did not look real and became even more surreal as he sat up and began speaking. Then my attention switched over to a woman rolling around on the ground about 20 yards away from him. Apparently the bullet bounced off of his face and landed in her hip. I read an account of the incident that was headlined "Woman Saved From Serious Bullet Wound By Girdle."

It turned out that the gunman was a recently fired employee and the man shot in the face at point blank range was his former boss. His wound proved to be non-life threatening and the assailant was convicted and went to prison.

The second violent use of a gun I witnessed occurred as I sat on the steps of the New York Public Library on 5TH Avenue between 40TH and 41ST Streets on a Saturday morning during my senior year of college. I was eating my Egg McMuffin before crossing the street to go to my new part time job. The quiet of the city was suddenly interrupted by a commotion in the doorway right in front of me on the corner of 40TH Street. Four young boys were running out of Lane Bryant, a woman's clothing store and running full speed towards 41ST Street. Suddenly, a man appeared out of the store and began screaming that they had just robbed the store. All of a sudden, one of the boys stopped, turned around and drew a pistol. He began firing at the man who quickly ducked back into the building. I sat there in disbelief as this shootout was unfolding right in front of my eyes. It never occurred to me to duck or run because it happened way too fast. As the boys turned off of 5TH Avenue onto 41St Street, the one with the gun tossed it into a doorway and kept on running.

By this point, there was already the wail of police sirens in response to the quick thinking store clerk having secretly stepped on the silent alarm button. Out of nowhere a police car roared down 5TH Avenue, ran the red light and slammed into a cab. Both of the vehicles were propelled onto the sidewalk across the street from me and everyone inside of both vehicles looked seriously injured. Soon about a dozen police cars screamed onto the scene and it was complete pandemonium. I ran across the street and pointed out the gun that the boy had tossed into the doorway. A policeman picked it up by using a pencil in the trigger guard, which I thought was such a cool, typical cop kind of a thing you would see on television. The cop was thanking me for pointing out where the gun was tossed when a police car pulled up with a young boy handcuffed in the back seat. The cop driving got out and violently dragged the boy out of the car. He pulled the screaming boy by his hair over to the ambulances that were loading up the cops and taxi driver injured in the car crash.

"Look what you did! You mother fucker. Look what you did!" he screamed just before he punched the handcuffed boy in the face and threw him back in the police car.

Let's not forget the time a drunken cop pulled a gun on me and some friends outside of a bar in South Orange, New Jersey or the time a drunken lunatic in a nightclub pulled out a gun claiming to be the reincarnation of the great writer, James Joyce.

But it is without a doubt my great privilege to wish the piece of garbage, poor excuse of a human being, who carjacked my wife at gunpoint a happy anniversary every year. As he sits and rots in prison, hopefully as somebody's bitch, my wife and I get to go on enjoying the fruits of freedom. So every year on the anniversary of his dastardly deed, I would like to remind him that we are free and he is in prison.

Yes, yes, yes. Guns are used in terrible crimes and the world would be a better place if there were no guns. But there are guns and that is the way it will always be. I have seen my fair share of the misuse of guns that have ended in tragedy. But then again, I have seen my fair share of the misuse of automobiles and alcohol that have ended in tragedy and I don't see anyone calling for the elimination of them.

The Day I Saw Evil

I went to bed on Monday, September 10TH with the usual dread of not being able to sleep, which I had grown so very accustom to over the last few months. I have this terrible habit of playing over and over in my head a nasty comment that was made to me or rewinding a horrible scene I watched on the evening news. It's kind of like this weird obsession that if I hear it or see it enough in my mind I will be able to alter the outcome of the event and rewrite the incident to a more satisfying conclusion. Anyone who has stuck their head in the fridge looking for a snack only to be disappointed at the lack of choices and then habitually goes back again and again every few minutes hoping the fridge got mysteriously filled with food knows what I am talking about.

I went to work the next morning with a list of tasks I wanted to accomplish. I sat in my office with a friendly cup of coffee and looked out my window at a beautiful sunny Tuesday morning when the phone rang.

"Dan, did you hear what happened?" asked Helene.

"What are you talking about?" I replied.

"A plane crashed into the World Trade Center," she replied.

"What?"

"A plane, a big one, crashed into the tower. They think a lot of people are dead. It's really horrible," she replied.

I signed onto America On Line and saw the first picture posted of the tower with the huge plume of black smoke rising from it.

"Oh my God. This is major, really major!" I exclaimed.

I said goodbye to Helene and turned on the radio. There was a flurry of newscasters giving minute-by-minute accounts of what was happening. I was still processing the fact that this terrible accident occurred when I heard a live account of a reporter screaming as the second plane slammed into the other tower. At that moment, I joined in the chilling chorus along with everyone else saying this was no accident. America was under an evil attack.

I called Helene back at her office and told her to get home. As we were speaking we were both simultaneously hearing reports that other planes were suspected to be hijacked and heading for possible suicide attacks. I told her that I wanted to, no, I had to, see what was going on and I would meet her back at the house. We live about thirty minutes outside of New York City and I knew that there was a spectacular view of Lower Manhattan from a nearby lookout at Eagle Rock Reservation in West Orange, NJ. I quickly ran to my car and flipped on the radio and began driving the few minutes to the lookout. On the way the radio reports were getting scarier and scarier. Another jet had just crashed into the Pentagon and there was a massive fire blazing. They were announcing that people were jumping from the burning towers, planes were heading possibly to crash into the Capital and other sites, everything was being evacuated, every firefighter and police officer were called to duty, the stock market was closed, fighter jets were scrambling.

Then came the words I will never forget as long as I live. The woman reporter was screaming on the radio.

"Oh my God, oh my God. The tower is coming down! The tower is crashing down!" were the words that literally announced a forever-new reality for everyone listening.

As I continued on towards the lookout I suddenly realized that everyone around me was in complete shock listening to their car radios. Many people had their hands over their mouths in disbelief, others were crying, most just had a zombie-like numbness expression on their faces. By the time I got within a few blocks of Eagle Rock Reservation, people were abandoning cars in the roadway and walking towards the lookout. As I approached the viewpoint, the faces of the people who were walking back from what I was about to see suddenly struck me. Every one of them had an expression that is forever etched in my memory. It was a look of helplessness, sorrow, shock and fear. Then I rounded the bend and became one of them.

I will not discuss what I saw when I rounded that bend for three reasons. The first reason is because it is a sacred memory that belongs only to me. We all have our own imprint of what transpired at that point in time, and I chose to keep mine private. The second reason I will not discuss it is because it is demeaning to the overwhelming tragedy of the event. Who really gives a damn how much of the horror I got to witness. It is not a point I wish to try to "one up" on others. The third reason is because I do not want to ever dignify the evil brought to our way of life that day by glorifying it with graphic details.

As I left the lookout, fresh with my new zombie face, I was suddenly snapped back to reality as an F-16 roared overhead. I kept thinking to myself how frustrated and disgusted the pilot must be that he is armed and ready with no target to shoot at and save America from this dastardly deed. I remember mumbling something about us being at war as I walked to my car with tears in my eyes. Just then the second tower collapsed.

The cell phones were useless, traffic was chaotic and all I could think about was getting home and making sure my family was safe. By the time I met Helene at the house, we began to sit in front of the TV and get introduced to the new reality we were living in. Lauren was still in school, which was a wise decision that the Board of Education made, since a number of the kids in the local high school had parents working in the towers and if they went home they might wait alone for their moms and dads who were never going to return.

The coming days had an eerie silence in the skies since their was no air traffic other then fighter planes and we, along with more people that will admit it, stocked up on food and supplies. This was done in case of a more devastating attack that could ruin our water, power, banking or worse, require us to flee our homes from an ensuing cloud of radioactive dust from a dirty bomb.

Since that awful time I have ventured back with my family to the lookout spot at Eagle Rock Reservation. It has become a permanent memorial site to the events of September 11TH, and the stone walls lining the viewing area are covered with flags, poems, letters and an assortment of other mementos relating to that fateful morning. I can't help but wonder if the peculiar silence that rumbles out of this almost holy spot is similar in tone and feeling to other areas that witnessed man's inhumanity towards man such as battlefields, concentration camps, or other genocidal sites. When the smoke and chaos dissipate leaving fading images and the distant echoes of screams, do the little children standing there holding their parents' hands on a sunny afternoon understand that they are only a moment away from the next cataclysmic event? From the sounds of their laughter and the sight of them romping around, I doubt it. Maybe we can learn something from them. Life goes on and we will eventually return to happier times.

We have all been touched in some way by evil and other negative forces. The lucky ones get to roll it off their backs or find some neat way to store it away into their lives like a well fitting piece of a jigsaw puzzle. The danger is to get too complacent about these negative forces and allow them to penetrate our vulnerable lives over and over again. Of course these things will undoubtedly happen again to us individually and collectively, but we will prevail and maintain the integrity of our lives by demonstrating the best response to evil is to be kind, compassionate but determined to defeat it. Those who perpetrate evil will eventually self-destruct like they always do. Like the Master Chitrabhanu of the Jainism sect of Hinduism professes, "Destructive thoughts are like bricks and become boomerangs."

Horse Tales

I have always considered myself to be an avid animal lover, but over the years I have had my loyalty tested with the great equestrians. My once objective, open mind and heart for this great beast has basically slammed closed with a permanent DO NOT DISTURB sign hanging from my door.

My first bad experience with a horse was back when I was in high school and I was driving my mother somewhere for lunch on a Saturday afternoon. We were on Pleasant Valley Way in West Orange, New Jersey, which was the road that inspired the song by Joni Mitchell. As we cruised down the road we were passing an area where there were stables.

Suddenly, I noticed a big brown horse a few hundred yards ahead of us rearing backwards, as a man was pulling on its reigns trying to keep it from backing into the busy road. I, along with all of the other cars, slowed down to watch and avoid smashing into it as it started to win the tug of war and stepped onto the road. As we pulled along side of the horse, it suddenly backed up further and its rear end thumped against the hood of my car. It's back legs folded and the horse was now sitting on my car!

My mother was grabbing my arm and hysterically screaming at me.

"Oh my God, do something… Ahhh!" she yelled.

She grabbed my arm and started frantically pulling at my shirt.

"What would you like me to do?" I shouted back as the car rocked from the weight of this true horse's ass.

Finally, the man pulling on the horse was joined by some others who eventually prevailed. They pulled the horse off of the car and back onto the grass. Amazingly, my car wasn't dented with the ass cheeks of a horse nor did it have a nice brown "racing stripe."

Strike one against horses.

A number of years later after graduating college I earned the dubious distinction of being one of the only living human beings to ever hit a horse on roller skates. Let me clarify that statement, I was wearing the roller skates, not the horse.

I was coerced into joining a very athletic girlfriend of mine to go roller-skating in Jockey Hollow National Park in Morristown, New Jersey. I had never been on roller skates before and she assured me that it would be fun and was perfectly safe. Like a total idiot, I believed her.

After I mastered the art of being able to stand on the skates without killing myself, I proceeded to follow her along a subtle upward inclined walking path. Others were chuckling as I stumbled by them with my arms flailing in the wind. I was so focused on every step I took that I didn't notice the incline leveled off and I was starting downhill. Before I knew it, I was picking up speed and roaring down the path to my doom.

My girlfriend stopped in response to my screams, and my last vision of her was her doubled over laughing as I zoomed past yelling something about my impending death and life being too short. Then it turned ugly.

I looked up and saw a policeman sitting on the biggest horse I had ever seen in my life standing sideways in my path. Right before impact I was consumed with thoughts of what I was going to be charged with if I survived. Then I slammed face first into the rock hard ribs of the horse.

As I was laying on the ground regaining my wits about me, I noticed a small crowd had gathered. As I looked up into their faces, I decided I wasn't too fond of horses.

Strike two against horses.

Now, skip ahead to 1990 and I've been with Helene for a year and change. Some friends invited us to join them for an event called the "Famous Night Ride." It was a horse tour through steep terrain and woods starting at dusk. Believe it or not, I agreed to go. I remember boring Helene with that stupid analogy about falling off the horse and getting right back on it.

There were about thirty relatively novice riders who had to be introduced to their companion horses. This was done by mounting each person on their horse and telling them to go into this corral to walk around for a while as the others were being mounted. For some reason, after I mounted, my horse decided to walk over to a small group of experienced riders who had their own horses and hang with them outside of the corral.

Suddenly, the group of experienced riders decided to take off in a full gallop and my horse decided to join them. It was one of the worst experiences of my life. We went from zero to full speed in an instant! I almost shit in my pants. We were roaring down this trail and my horse decided to start biting the horse next to him. The other horse responded by trying to kick me off of my horse. I had no idea of how to control the horse and was hanging on for dear life. I started pulling on its ears and smacking it on the head. It was impervious to my demands. By the time the horse stopped we were out of sight of the main group and everyone I knew. I was ready to jump off of this stupid creature, kick it in the ass and walk home.

As Helene and our friends caught up to me, they unfortunately convinced me to continue with what would ultimately come to be known as The Hell Ride.

As dusk slipped into darkness our group of thirty or so riders proceeded to stumble and bump through the unforgiving terrain. It was so dark you couldn't see your own hand in front of your face or the branches that were poking you in the eyes. Suddenly, I heard Helene screaming for help ahead of me. As I came upon her, or at least I think I was upon her but it was too dark to be sure, her horse was rearing back on its hind legs. She yelled for help but my horse refused to stop and just clip-clopped by her.

After we survived the balance of our wonderful journey with these four-legged fiends we were invited to a barbecue sponsored by the tour leaders. It consisted of ex-convicts flipping hamburgers with their bare hands and singing X-rated cowboy songs.

Strike three, the horse is out!

Winter Camping

Throughout our illustrious camping experiences, my friend Dave and I always felt that the world was not only a forgiving place, but a warm and friendly place as well. That all changed when we decided to go winter camping in Canada.

We had the notion that it would be a thrill to spend the first week in January of 1976 perched in some remote area covered with a fresh blanket of new snow. We set out in my parents' 1971 Vega Hatchback, heading north looking for a snowstorm, after my parents specifically instructed me not to take the car anywhere. Since they were vacationing in Florida, I figured they would never find out. We drove and drove up through New England and didn't find any snowy weather. As the hours wore on it got colder and colder, but there were no snowstorms in sight. After about 8 hours of driving, it was well into the evening and we were approaching the Canadian boarder. We decided to keep going, no matter how long it took, until we found snow falling from the sky.

We pulled up to the lonely customs building at the Canadian boarder somewhere in New Hampshire and had to wait for someone to even realize that we were there. I guess they were not too concerned with terrorists or smugglers going into Canada back in those days. When we finally got the attention of the boarder guard, he asked us for our proof of citizenship, so we politely showed it to him. Everything was going fine until he asked us some routine questions. I was in dumbfounded when Dave stumbled on the answer to the question, "Where were you born?" Well, after we were searched, our car was basically dismantled and left in a heap in a nearby garage. Our once neatly packed camping equipment was now strewn all over the place and we were told that we could be on our way. As we were trying to put all of our stuff back together, I laughed as I looked up and saw a sign that said "Welcome to Canada."

By mid morning the next day we decided that we better make a decision to stop and camp somewhere or we might end up at the North Pole before we found fresh snow. We had wandered to a deserted skiing area north of St. Anne De Beaupre and scoped out the surrounding mountains. It was extraordinarily cold, somewhere in the order of 20 to 30 below zero on this crisp, blue morning. It looked harmless enough. So even though there was no fresh snow, we decided to start climbing until we found an appropriate place to set up camp.

After loading up our gear, we started hiking towards a clearing that looked like it would lead us up one of the taller mountains and we started to hear French speaking voices. They turned out to be the skeleton crew of the ski area doing some maintenance work. We tried to explain to them that we were going camping and quickly realized that their English was worse that our French. Eventually we got our point across and they told us it was stupid to try to brave the elements up there. In fact, the reason the ski area was closed was due to the dangerously cold weather. It was going to drop to70 below zero and would be deadly cold. We simply replied with an enthusiastic cheer! The people tried to talk us out of going, but after all, we were invincible!

Dave and I hiked about 1,500 feet higher in elevation in the next few hours. Our lungs were burning from the cold and we were disoriented from the climb. We decided to set up camp in a clearing that consisted of packed ice and offered no insulation. We set up our thin spring tent, bundled up and crawled inside it in the afternoon for what was going to be a very long night. By early evening, it was getting dark and the cold was becoming painfully real. It was no warmer than 20 below zero inside the tent and we were starting to realize that we made a dreadful mistake by venturing up this mountain.

There was absolutely nothing to do except to try not to shiver and lose more body heat. It was impossible to eat and all of our liquid was freezing so we were really thirsty. We had no firewood and were unable to start a fire to keep ourselves warm. Dave handed me a 5 foot length of rubber tube that we had brought along so we could each devise a make shift breathing apparatus. By sticking the tubing up our pant legs and running it under our clothes and out our shirts into our mouths, we could warm up the air going into our lungs. This made it possible to breath without the painful burning from the cold air.

Now it was time to keep from falling asleep and drifting into hypothermia and eventually, death.

As I stood outside my dorm room and looked up, I watched as one of my roommates fell from our third floor window and splattered face first onto the pavement in front of me! Suddenly I woke up realizing that I had fallen asleep, had a nightmare and was back on the mountain. I still had the tube in my mouth and was shivering, so I knew I was alive. As I looked over at Dave, I saw his face encased in a sparkling glitter of frost, the kind of frost you would find on an old piece of meat in the freezer. His tube had fallen from his mouth and the moisture from his breath had frozen to his face. I woke him up and he began to panic.

"We have to get out of here! We're going to die if we stay here!" he screamed.

I had to scream back at him to calm him down. If we stepped out of our tent, we probably would never have lived to see another day.

As the Canadian midnight wore on, it was deceptively light outside. You could easily wear sunglasses from the brightness of the moon and stars. But this was Mother Nature fooling us into thinking it was safe out there. The quick snap of trees cracking from the cold reminded us of what awaited us if we wanted to prove that we could be even stupider than we already were. The only sounds of life that we heard were eerie hooting sounds that I still want to believe were owls.

At the first break of daylight we heard the muffled sound of a helicopter echoing through the mountains. Gee, wouldn't it be nice if they were coming to rescue us, I thought. It kept getting closer and closer until it was right over us creating one hell of a wind. Dave and I were screaming to each other as we scrambled outside to see what was happening. As the helicopter hovered above, the pilot was looking for a place to land and pick us up. They were screaming to us though a PA system in French but we couldn't make out the words. After a few futile attempts the helicopter left. They couldn't get to us. Now we were really scared.

Our fear turned into determination and we made a bold decision to abandon most of our gear and hightail it down the mountain. Keep in mind that we could barely walk, breath or think by this point. I truly believe that this was our last chance to get out or else die.

After what seemed like an eternity we made it down the mountain to an awaiting welcome party made up of a few people happy to see us, and others who wanted to kick our sorry asses for putting them in danger by having to attempt to rescue us. We were treated in their infirmary and left the area without a good amount of our equipment. It was all still on top of the mountain entombed in the ferocious cold.

The Vega had to be jump started because the cold had sapped the battery's power. It's amazing that the aluminum engine under that tin hood didn't just explode from the frigid temperatures. As the car limped out of the area we couldn't touch the windows or our skin would stick to them from the cold. We headed south and ended up at a quirky little bed and breakfast in Quebec City, where we heated up cans of beans under the hot water tap and played Frisbee in the snow. We were thankful to be back in civilization. Then we celebrated by going to a diner and getting a *real* hot meal. Unbeknownst to us there are a lot of Quebec residents that don't like Americans. This became apparent when a bunch of guys came up to us in the diner and started giving us grief in French. Dave and I mistook their threats for friendly chitchat and started laughing. One of these guys cleared up our confusion by knocking me off my chair.

We couldn't get out of Canada fast enough. The next day as we headed home we made a pit stop in Bridgeport Connecticut. Dave and I were in tee shirts as we walked around. I looked up at a bank thermometer and realized that it was only 35 degrees. It was amazing to think that we had just come from camping in weather that was 100 degrees colder and we were alive to talk about it.

My parents were pissed that I took the Vega without their permission, the customs people didn't like us very much, the people at the mountain hated our guts, I got assaulted by the Quebec City Welcoming Committee in a diner, we lost all of our camping equipment and we almost died. I think that's when I started wanting my vacations to be in hotels surrounded by palm trees.

Dwellings

If it is true that we are products of our environments, then my home environment manufactured me into a naive, trusting soul when I left home and ventured out into the world. My upbringing nurtured my creativity, molded me into trusting people and cradled me into the lullaby that nothing bad could ever happen to me. When I think of my childhood home, visions of clean sheets, warm meals, interested parents and virtually no worries come to mind.

College was my first out of home and, sometimes, out of body experience. I had room and board provided by my folks and had the very simple responsibility of going to classes and staying alive. I stumbled through these two assignments, nearly failing at both on a number of occasions. If it wasn't for the fact that I had an actual address, I would have been pretty good at being a nomad. I was accustomed to waking up in unfamiliar bedrooms, or in my bed with unfamiliar companions. Remember, this was pre-Aids times and life was a lot simpler in this department.

I lived in a perpetually smelly apartment that was on campus. It had a carpet that had enough food ground into it to feed an army and a kitchen sink buried under weeks of moldy dishes. We had gotten a puppy named Jerry, named after our savior Jerry Garcia, who routinely used the place as her toilet. Despite all of this gross stuff, the traffic of women flowing in and out of our apartment was very high, as were we most of the time.

I lived most of my college career with a good friend and roommate named Eric. He was a very bright, adventurous guy who had the temper of a rubber band ready to snap. We journeyed through those tumultuous four years laughing, partying, brawling, screwing and learning a lot. In the end when the smoke cleared, we left college with the same vacant look in our eyes that you might expect to see in soldiers returning from the horrors of war. We were smarter, tougher and had lost what was left of our innocence.

I moved back with my folks for a while and dedicated myself to the band. I had moved down to the basement for some privacy and chose to live as a temporary boarder. The sublime urchin life in the murky basement seemed to be a fitting testament to my life. Also, it worked out better with my late night schedule to slither into the basement instead of stumbling up the stairs and having to confront my mom and dad. This worked out until John Lennon was murdered.

On the night Lennon was shot by Mark David Chapman, I was heading into New York City with some band members to speak with the owner of a great Greenwich Village club called Kenny's Castaways. The club was a place that launched the careers of many famous musicians and was a regular hangout for many celebrities. I relentlessly annoyed the owner for months until he reluctantly let us play in his club. We ended up playing there a bunch of times and he was starting to actually believe that we were pretty good. This particular night we were going to meet him to consummate a deal to open up for some major acts in his club. When we arrived into Greenwich Village, people were hugging and crying on the streets having just been stunned by the news of John Lennon's murder. Apparently, Lennon had been friends with the owner and was often seen in the club, so he was furious at us when we broached the subject of business that night. After he threw us out, we licked our wounds and limped home that night never to play there again.

When I woke up, I was humiliated and embarrassed by my behavior towards the club owner. I needed to be embraced and consoled as I agreed to go out to breakfast at a diner with my mom and dad. I explained to them that I would go, but had to be back by a certain time to retreat to the basement and participate in a ten-minute moment of silence that was going to take place in John Lennon's memory. It was to be accompanied by the piano playing of Davis Sanchez and broadcast live on a major New York radio station.

We went to the diner and it was getting late when I reminded them that I had to be home. As we got in the car my dad was getting annoyed.

"What's with all of this sudden devotion towards John Lennon? I haven't heard you even mention his name in years?" he said in a very challenging tone.

He went on to question my sincerity and suggested that my grieving was a bunch of bullshit. I got furious at him and a major argument erupted. It ended with me punching the dashboard of his car so hard that I cracked it. When we got home my dad told me to pack up and get the hell out of the house.

I showed up at the apartment of one of my band members and his girlfriend asking for a place to stay for "a little while." I ended up living on the futon in their living room for three months until they couldn't deal with me anymore. So back to mom and dad's once again after making peace with them.

There is nothing to make you feel more like a total loser that to be in your mid-twenties and picking up girls saying "Hey, lets go back to my mom and dad's house!" I guess there must have been a lot of losers where I lived.

My next dwelling was a beautiful house in the rural suburbs of Morris County, New Jersey. I ended up renting it with three local friends. It was on a nice piece of property and had a huge finished basement for the band to use for rehearsals. The house turned into a party factory and was usually filled with throngs of people. As the band became more and more popular the parties grew in size. It got to the point where we would have tons of strangers showing up on weekends. After a while, we had to tone it down or we were going to be evicted. It returned to being a lot of fun, fairly comfortable and relatively clean.

It was during this time that I met a really screwed up girl, who was a struggling model in New York. To this day I refer to her as The Mistake. I made the big blunder of leaving the house in Morris County and moving in with The Mistake in New York on 23RD Street. We lived right next door to the Chelsea Hotel, where Sid Vicious had been murdered. Our building was made up of whores, drug dealers and struggling musicians and models. One of the struggling musicians in our building was Peter Tork from the Monkees. He had regained the status as "struggling" musician and fit right in with us and the other tenants. Another resident was a pimp named Sam, who lived a floor below us with his three "wives." Boy, this place sure was different than the suburbs of New Jersey.

On the street, the whores didn't bother hitting on the local musicians because they knew we had no money to spend. The drug dealers left the residents alone, too. There was a certain "don't shit where you eat" understanding. You could approach them, but they wouldn't bother you. In the middle of a concrete, screaming city, this understanding kept our little neighborhood fairly civil. I would retreat into the apartment for peace and quite, as opposed to being in New Jersey and running outside to find privacy. This lifestyle took a lot of getting used to and I only lasted about a year. The Mistake and I decided to move back to the Maplewood area.

We moved to a dilapidated tenement a few towns over from Maplewood and lived a fairly miserable existence. Finally, the place burned to the ground in a fire that some blamed on faulty wiring and others blamed on my poor judgment by overloading the sockets with too many plugs. We stayed with friends while we were figuring out what to do, and it was during this time that I found out The Mistake was having an affair with my dear friend, Peter. I threw in the towel and moved, where else, back in with mom and dad!

Down and out, I was in a local bar one night with the usual cast of characters when I was introduced to a very charismatic foreigner named Alex. He was the son of two college professors from Yugoslavia and was in America to take it by storm. We debated politics, religion and communism, got drunk, woke up and were living together in his miniature house that was about the size of a Volvo.

Never in my life have I seen more women be uncontrollably attracted to someone for no apparent reason. He was the unbathed flame and they were the moths with no sense of smell. This created a lot of female surplus that I benefited from. Alex would have sex with anything that moved, he had no scruples… none! His criteria was simple, a girl must have most of her limbs, a pulse and be breathing. If so, she passed the test and was going to be a conquest of his. He would be with a knock out beautiful girl one day and a gross pig the next. He didn't care and was equally proud of both, even if he couldn't remember their names.

Despite his smell, he was the breath of fresh air that I needed to jump-start my life. Alex looked at crap and saw opportunity. He could bullshit his way into the Oval Office and make strategic decisions with the President if he had felt like it. He was so good at connecting with people and making things happen. He managed to befriend a certain someone who was responsible for creating fiber optics. Alex would come back from hanging out with this guy and be filled with all kinds of ideas that he had copped from his newfound friend and he could capitalize on. The older man took Alex under his wing as a son and even invited him to his daughters wedding. This turned into a disaster when the family had the wedding pictures developed from the disposable cameras that were passed around to the guests. Alex had taken one of the cameras into the bathroom along with this guy's other daughter and took all kinds of obscene action photos of the two of them together. He wasn't invited back to their house anymore.

On another occasion, he forged a guess pass and press credentials for the Bicentennial celebrations in New York and was seen having dinner with Dan Rather at an exclusive press party. Then there was the time we were boarding an airplane and he decided to head into the cockpit. Anyone else would have been arrested, but not Alex. He ended up having a private tour.

Finally he got bored with this area and moved into Manhattan for greater adventures. I once again dwelled with my folks as I opened my video store and he moved into a church and opened a 1950's memorabilia shop in Lower Manhattan. Yes, he moved into a church, and the funny part was the church didn't allow him to bring in any women. The Yugoslavian priest who had befriended Alex and gave him shelter in the church made him promise to uphold the "no girl" rule. I think Alex kept his word for a week or two, but the priest never found out. Amongst his inventory in his memorabilia store, Alex had a huge refrigerator magnet collection that grew into the worlds largest. He went on tour with it and received critical acclaim. Who else could take those stupid little things that hold up grocery lists and photos and turn it into a goldmine?

At last conversation, Alex had convinced a certain think tank at a major university that he was some kind of expert in super magnetics. They ended up funding a "project" of his and he was then recognized as a leading authority on this subject.

Then I was introduced to a guy named Steve who seemed pretty together except for the fact that he was also living in his parents' basement. We rented a house in Maplewood and proceeded to promptly destroy it in every way imaginable. The landlord lived two doors away and routinely freaked out as he watched his hard efforts turn into all night parties, visits by the police, garbage throughout the house and outrageous behavior. We joined forces with a friend who lived around the corner and had a great swimming pool that turned into the place we would end up when the bars closed. It was not uncommon to see drunken idiots and topless girls scurrying between our two castles in the late night hours.

One night, after finishing a dinner I had prepared for a girl I was trying to impress, I insisted that she stay put, as I would do the dishes. I did what was typical for our house after dinner. I opened the door, grabbed the dishes one by one, and flung them like Frisbees into the brook behind our house. I guess she wasn't impressed because she didn't even stick around for dessert.

Soon I was introduced to this older woman who had a four-year-old child and was going through a divorce. The first few weeks of our relationship took me to her established, clean world complete with a nice home and responsible friends. Finally, I invited her over to my war torn, dilapidated world. Thirteen years later, she still reminds me of how she silently freaked out then over the filth and stench of my home. She has had plenty of time to remind me of those days, because we have never been apart since then and she is now my wife, Helene.

After Helene saw the conditions I was living in, and the people I was hanging out with, she encouraged me to move out of Maplewood for both of our sakes. At her suggestion, I answered an ad for a one-bedroom residence connected to a farmhouse about an hour from Maplewood. It turned out to be the adjoining servant quarters of a residence built in the 1750's and was fully restored and maintained by a 78-year-old woman named Mrs. Bartell. I jumped at the opportunity, rented the place and that is when my life began to turn around.

Mrs. Bartell would be up everyday with the sun and out in the fields on her tractor. She would greet me in the evenings with her boyfriend and their half finished bottle of bourbon. Often she would have bags of fresh picked tomatoes, cucumbers, squash and more waiting for me at my doorstep. I kept my home spotless and everything was always in order. I loved my neatly filled bedroom closet so much, that I would keep the closet door open just so I could look at it. Every night I would cook a full meal with a meat, vegetable and pasta. This was a new type of life for me and I fell in love with it quickly.

The partying stopped soon after I moved in with Mrs. Bartell and has never resumed. I found life to be a hell of a lot more rewarding this way. The tragic side of this transformation in my life began when

I realized that none of my supposed friends in Maplewood would even come up to visit me in my new life. They abandoned me and went on about their business. To this day I'm not sure if I threatened them, bored them or they were just too dysfunctional to even care. But it doesn't matter, because I found my way out. I know that if I had not made the bold move to escape the degrading life I was leading, I would have died in Maplewood.

After two years, I moved in with Helene and Lauren, and our life as a family began. Since then, we have bought our own home and are hardworking, family oriented people.

"Can you even believe that you used to live like that?" Helene asked me the other night.

"Of course I can. I can still smell the stench and see the dirt and mess like it was yesterday," I said without hesitation.

I don't want to forget those days, they were very important in my life. If it wasn't for stopping and seeking shelter in all of those dwellings along my journey I don't know where I would have ended up. Now, as I look back I am thankful I got to where I am, regardless of the route I took to get here.

Who's Up There?

In 1978, the summer before I graduated from college, I came back to Maplewood to stay with my folks and was either rehearsing with my band or performing just about every night. There was a great deal of attention being paid to northern New Jersey in those days regarding outrageous reports of UFO sightings. It was making headlines in the newspapers on a regular basis and drawing acknowledgement on the evening news. Everything from reports of the stereotypical lights in the sky to actual eyewitness accounts of unexplained crafts in broad daylight regularly were broadcast on our televisions. It seemed like everyone either had a first hand encounter or knew someone who had an extra terrestrial experience. It was kind of similar to living in New Jersey and having a Bruce Springsteen tale, you either had your own personal Bruce story or knew someone who did.

Since the days of Roswell, New Mexico and all that Area 51 stuff, it seems that every now and then a certain area was the latest hot bed of UFO hysteria. The flurry of supposed sightings would escalate for a while and gradually drift off to another part of the country. I guess it was just our turn to be entertained and terrorized with these out of the world possibilities. At first, most of the people were pretty nonchalant about the whole thing, but as it started to pick up steam it got fairly serious, and usually apathetic citizens started speaking out demanding answers.

I've always been of the belief that it is highly improbable that we are alone in the universe. I have often thought that if humans are the best things that the cosmos could come up with, it was pretty pathetic. But I also realized that it is unlikely that we have been in direct contact with intelligent life from other planets, and since no one had ever gotten their hands on any concrete evidence, I remained skeptical. I have felt all along that viewing blurry pictures and shaky video of alleged spacecraft was less than solid proof. If anyone ever took me for a ride in a spacecraft or showed me an alien they would have my full attention.

My apathy and cynicism was turned to awe by a traffic-stopping event that took place in Maplewood one night that summer. I didn't witness this event, but spoke to a number of credible people who did observe the legendary encounter. What I witnessed was the mysterious and bizarre response of the government to demands of an explanation by the residents of our town.

A typical summer weekday in Maplewood was winding down as people were barbecuing, walking their dogs and washing their cars. Suddenly there was a wave of commotion as people started to hurry down the street towards some kind of disturbance. I was told that it was the kind of response people might give as if hearing there had been a car accident or there was a fight going on in the park. As more and more people moved towards the cause of the disturbance, a decent size crowd started to form at the intersection of two major cross streets. Rob, a friend of mine who was in the crowd, said that as he came within a block of the spectacle, his attention was drawn up just above the tree tops by glimpses of a glittering metallic surface he could see through the trees and the rooftops. As he got closer, he found himself standing under a cigar shaped object about the size of a football field, no more than 100 feet above the crowd, and amazingly silent. My friend's mother told me that the visible underside of this object was perfectly smooth like an egg, with no seams or rivets. By everyone's account it had no windows or doors, it was just a gigantic metal object that was silently hovering within the view of hundreds of people. The only noticeable feature on this thing was a series of flashing lights that were around the circumference of this oblong object. All of this chaos prompted dozens of calls to the local police department, so there were also plenty of cops in the crowd as witnesses.

After ten to fifteen minutes, it slowly started to move upward and suddenly zipped away at incredible speed. People were stunned and confused as to what had just happened to them. As you can imagine, there was plenty to talk about when the sun came up! Little did they know how confusing it was about to get.

Within one day, the story was plastered all over every major New York area TV station. Remember, this was against the backdrop of months and months of other UFO reports in the local area. Well, apparently public demand for answers became tremendous and the media was relentless. Apparently, this thing had been seen by thousands of people in a bunch of neighboring communities and the public had enough. It was even picked up by the air traffic controllers on radar at the Newark Airport, which was about five miles away. Finally, about two weeks after the incident in Maplewood, a town meeting was called at the request of the United States Air Force in response to the people's demand for some answers. I clearly remember how intense it was to see this happening right where I live, involving people that I grew up with. This was for real; you could touch it, feel it and smell it. It is very sobering to see an event like this up close and personal, as opposed to seeing it on the news or reading about it in the paper.

I went to the standing room only town meeting with some friends of mine and immediately noticed that there were all kinds of NBC, CBS and ABC news trucks outside along with many local stations. I thought it was really impressive to see reporters that I watched every night jockeying for position in the meeting, and just as interested in getting answers as we all were. Also, there were all kinds of, what I would guess were, FBI or secret service type characters milling around taking pictures of the crowd. What was going on here?

The mayor nervously spoke along with some other local politicians and then they turned the floor over to the Air Force people. They quickly, and tactlessly, tried to tell everyone that what they had witnessed was a weather balloon and the crowd got infuriated. Some folks were yelling at these clowns and everyone was obviously insulted by this lame suggestion. People were walking up to microphones that were set up to allow for the audience to speak and firing questions back to the Air force spokespeople.

"How does a weather balloon appear and suddenly take off at hundreds of miles an hour?" asked one citizen.

The Air Force had no answer. When someone asked what was the source of this supposed weather balloon and where was it from, they also had no response. It went on like this until the residents realized that this meeting was a waste of time, and no truth would be found that night.

This situation was never resolved and after a few more legendary incidents, the sightings suddenly stopped. People talked about these events for a few years and, after a while, most of the witnesses found a comfortable place to park their memories. As the years have marched on, I have conjured up my own ideas as to what really happened that summer in Maplewood. I believe that the government knew exactly what happened because I believe that they were responsible for the spectacular incident over the treetops in our town. From Roswell, New Mexico to Maplewood New Jersey and everywhere in between the United States has probably perpetrated the biggest hoax in the history of the modern world.

Starting with the simple premise of our government wanting its enemies to believe that they were in possession of some out of this world technologies salvaged from some intergalactic fender bender in the deserts of New Mexico, and having the need to continuously fuel this charade to keep our adversaries guessing, our government has schemed to extraordinary lengths to make the unbelievable into reality. What better way to keep one's opponents at bay, than to make them wonder if you are in possession of bigger and better weapons than they possess. And what better way to make them think you have such weapons, than to convince them you acquired them from the leftovers of an alien smash-up in your back yard. Thus the creation of the Area 51 myths and the endless stream of UFO's buzzing around, that turns out to be nothing more than super hi-tech man made props. Of course, the only way to make this hoax complete is to keep everyone in the dark, even the loyal American masses. In fact, our government has probably even gone through the elaborate exercise of terrorizing "eyewitnesses" with visits from the Men In Black types. No, I don't mean having Will Smith and Tommy Lee Jones dropping by, but instead having a knock on the door and threatening warnings by pale-faced drones in trench coats urging witnesses to forget what they saw. People wouldn't threaten you unless you saw something they want you to believe you shouldn't have seen.

The hoax is completed by the vehement denials of the government knowing anything about captured UFO's or involvement with aircraft mistaken for UFO's. The United States even went to the lengths of having its own UFO Blue Book project commissioned to study the phenomenon for many years. What a great way to look like they were sincerely searching for the truth. How ironic that they had it all along.

Employment

You might think that someone of my stature as an owner of a technical recruiting firm would be compassionate to the plight of the employed, and sometimes unemployed. The mere fact that over the years I have counseled countless candidates, negotiated exotic compensation packages and handheld people and their families through all kinds of relocation traumas would keep me in touch with the realities of how harsh and frightening a business world it can be out there. You might think…

The unfortunate truth is that I find myself forever slipping into the same unmerciful spiral that many potential employers fall into, judging a book by its cover. If I see a resume of an individual that has had many different jobs in a short period of time, I tend to immediately label the individual a "job hopper." If I see a graduation date going back before a certain year, I begin to think that they might be too old for the job. What really sucks is lately I have been instinctively classifying people as being over the hill and then realize that they are younger than me! That really hurts.

This whole thing has me realizing that I am living in a glass house with a big pile of rocks that I am always ready to throw. I think a little retrospective of my work history would be a good reminder in how to be compassionate. Imagine a person's resume that included newspaper delivery boy, house painter, bus boy, golf caddie, liquor store clerk, ladies shoe store clerk, valet parking attendant, musician el fartacious, pool builder, ski lift attendant, ski shop manager, yogurt store manager, fine menswear salesman, shoe salesman, hardware store salesman, musician el strugglino, delivery man, gynecologist (only kidding), deposition editor for the Agent Orange litigation, mail room manager, insurance salesman, wholesale meat salesman, skating store salesman, wood burning stove store helper, recording studio flunky, musician de sortofsuccessfulo, video store owner, recruiter and a whole bunch that I simply can't, or don't want to remember. Well, that is what my resume would include. How far do you think I would get in the business world?

Now, I know that I am a productive member of society and have a wealth of ideas and energy to share. In fact, I always have been that kind of person. But do you really think that someone looking at my work history would take me seriously? Maybe after they got finished laughing and passing my resume around the office for everyone's amusement, but I kind of doubt it. Every person has a story, that is, a true story. Not the neatly packaged bullshit that we dress ourselves up as on our resumes, but the real history of events that have led them to where they are today. Unfortunately, not too many people seem to have the time or desire to sincerely listen to a person's true story. We are all too busy with deadlines, quotas and other business commitments to consider anyone who has the slightest blemish in their professional background. So we force people to overstate, omit, mislead and circumvent aspects of their lives in order to survive. It is not the fault of the candidate, but the fault of the people who judge the resume of the candidate. Show me a resume that even slightly deviates from the normal pattern and I will show you a person who will have a difficult time getting an interview.

So what is the answer to this problem? Should a person lie and be dishonest in order to get a job and hope that they don't get caught? Should the responsibility be more on the part of employers to be compassionate and see if a person's job-hopping like leapfrog was due to justifiable causes? I think the solution is a person must do what they can feel comfortable with answering to in life. The truth might cost you a job now, but a lie might cost you the job, or your dignity, later. Sorry no easy answer, just a difficult question.

I guess I am lucky that my boss never asked *me* for my resume.

About the Author

Dan Bruder has been an author and composer for the last three decades, having compiled a significant collection of works that are tributes to his rich life experiences. He spent the first half of his adult life as a rock performer and was mentored by, worked with, or opened onstage for, many music industry legends. His fans and friends always viewed him as a loveable, energetic, outspoken hurricane of creativity. But his entertaining came with a personal price that became too much for him to bear. After chasing the rock and roll dream for many years, he came close to the edge of ruin through self-abuse and over indulgence.

In the mid 1980's, Bruder turned his energies away from the music business and live performing, and settled into a comfortable, married life. During this period he became a successful executive recruiter and once again the creative juices began to flow. Retooling his song writing talents to develop short stories, he ventured onto a journey of self-exploration. The result has been a series of autobiographical tales that are truthful accounts and admissions of his adventures.

Bruder earned a B.A from Fairleigh Dickenson University and has written articles for various magazines and journals. He lives in New Jersey with his wife and stepdaughter.

Printed in the United States
971600001B

9 781403 360793